DALEY'S LA

'Ignorance of the law
that — of all people. I think I'll have to
He moved nearer to Arthur, a sardonic smile on his face.

Arthur looked desperate and gabbled, 'Mister Chisholm — be fair. I'm a victim of circumstances. I've been turned over by some nasty little villain who has exploited my gullibility.' There was sweat standing out on his forehead and he absentmindedly mopped at it with a silk handkerchief.

'Feeling warm, Arthur?' asked Chisholm.

'It's a little close in here, Mister Chisholm. I've told Dave he always keeps his place too hot.'

'I've got a place where we can cool you down, Arthur. It's called the nick.'

Also by Anthony Masters in Sphere Books:

MINDER

Minder – Back Again

ANTHONY MASTERS

Based on the Minder series created by Leon Griffiths
and on the scripts written by Leon Griffiths

SPHERE BOOKS LIMITED
London and Sydney

First published in Great Britain by
Sphere Books Ltd 1984
30-32 Gray's Inn Road, London WC1X 8JL

TRADE
MARK

Set in Century Schoolbook

Printed and bound in Great Britain by
Cox & Wyman Ltd, Reading

Publisher's Note

Minder – Back Again

PART ONE

Terry had jogged four miles when he heard the shout. He paused, panting, trying to make out who the hell it was. Terry didn't feel like company – he just felt like collapsing on his bed with a nice cup of tea.

'I've been trying to get hold of you for days.'

'Well – if it isn't Justin James,' said Terry sourly. He was confronted by a good looking brash young man, exuding considerable nervous energy and standing outside a greengrocer's shop as if he owned it.

'Where is he?'

'Who?'

'The great man. Signor Corleone. *Numero Uno*. Daley.'

'Oh, 'im.'

'He's giving me a blank.'

'So what's new?'

A housewife was inspecting the fruit and vegetables just behind Justin.

'Sprouts are beautiful,' he said. 'Fresh today – straight off the boat.' Justin returned his gaze to Terry. 'Where is he then? He's never at home, the lock-up's engaged all the time. I belled him at the Winchester, but he weren't there neither.'

'He must have gone invisible,' said Terry, wondering how he was going to get away from Justin. But Justin was persistent.

'You look knackered.'

'Thanks.'

'Jogging?'

'No – I'm body popping.'

'Funny man.'

'What do you want to see Arthur for?'

'I want to see him because we're all gonna be rich.' He picked up a nectarine and gave it to Terry. 'These are lovely.' Then his voice became confidential. 'Tickets. *Capisce*? This is the big one, Tel.'

'Is it?' Terry bit thirstily into the nectarine.

'I've been working on it for weeks. Arthur would be very impressed.'

'He's only impressed by one thing.'

'Yeah – that's what I'm on about. Money in the bank. But it's too big for me, see. He's got muscle.'

'Arthur!'

'Well – he's got you.'

'He's not a gangster, you know,' said Terry, enjoying the nectarine. 'He's a name – he's a face.'

Suddenly the greengrocer appeared behind Justin. 'That'll be twenty-five pence.'

'What?'

'Twenty-five pence,' he repeated firmly.

'Look here,' said Terry indignantly. 'I thought you worked in this joint.' But Julian was otherwise occupied with the greengrocer. Grudgingly he handed him the twenty-five pence and then turned back to the woman who was just about to enter the shop.

'Don't go in there, love,' said Justin. 'They're robbers.'

The greengrocer took immediate exception to that comment. 'Shove off or I'll chin you.'

Justin took a step back. 'Don't start on me, mate. If you're looking for trouble, I've got the right man here.'

Terry grabbed Justin's arm. 'Behave yourself.' He smiled warily at the greengrocer. 'Sorry pal – he hasn't had his breakfast yet.'

None too gently, Terry steered Justin away from the shop. 'You've got more front than the Albert Hall,' he told him.

Justin treated Terry to a lovely, wide smile. 'I get by though, don't I?'

Strolling towards Terry's flat, Justin expanded on his scheme. 'We can take over – we can break the monopoly. Of course, I'm not just talking about football – it could be anything – Wimbledon, Covent Garden Ballet, Chelsea Flower Show, boxing – the sky's the limit.'

'And what do you think Little Phil, King of the Touts, will do? Abdicate?'

'He's had a good run. The king is dead – long live the king. I'm gonna get my act together when I'm away.'

'Where're you going?'

'Inside.'

'That's nice.'

'I'm on bail – didn't you know? Crown Court next week. Me brief reckons six months. No problem.'

'That's good to hear.'

'It's an open nick. Be a doddle. That's why I want to settle up the tickets thing.'

'So you can get another stretch when you come out?'

'That's what I'm trying to tell you – it's legal. They advertise in *The Times*, don't they? Wait till Arthur hears about this – he'll be over the moon.'

'He usually is,' said Terry dourly as he passed a man with a briefcase coming out of his block of flats. Then the man stopped and said:

'Mr McCann?'

'Maybe.'

'You're a difficult man to get hold of.'

'What name did you say?' Justin asked with mock innocence.

'McCann.'

'Nobody of that name lives round here.'

But Terry intervened quickly. 'Leave it out, Justin. I am over twenty-one. What's your problem, pal?'

The man gave Terry an envelope. 'We have written to you several times, sir – but what with the post these days. . . So the office decided a letter by hand would be better.'

'I'm honoured.'

'It's all self-explanatory. Good morning.'

He hurried away, leaving Terry curiously opening the letter. Justin read it over his shoulder. 'Don't stand for that,' he said.

'No?'

'I mean – the income tax people can't *do* that. Give 'em a blank – you're not –'

'Justin?'

'Yeah?'

'What's the Italian for "shut up"?'

'I'm only trying to help.' He sounded aggrieved.

'Yeah – I understand that,' said Terry. 'But you give me a headache. *Comprendo*? *Ciao*, Justin.'

Terry walked stiffly towards his front door but Justin dashed after him. 'What about Daley?'

'Send me a letter – by hand.'

'Come on, Tel. I've gotta see him. You promised.'

Terry put the key in the lock, but Justin persisted, 'You'll be seeing him later. What about lunch? All down to me.'

'Don't give me lunch, mate. You had a hard time paying twenty-five pence for a nectarine.'

'I got dough.'

'Yeah?'

'Yeah – course I have. Me and Daley – you gotta understand, Tel – we're made for each other.'

'You are?'

'The young tiger and the old fox. And we're *all* gonna earn out of it.' He drew Terry in, anxious that he shouldn't think he was being left out. 'I'll book a table at Mario's. I mean – Arthur eats, doesn't he? Tel, doesn't he? Tel –'

Terry propped himself up on the doorpost, more exhausted by Justin than his jog. 'OK.'

'You'll fix it?' Justin looked at him with wide-eyed enthusiasm and Terry felt even more drained.

'I'll phone you.'

'If I don't hear from you – it's on.'

'You'll be at your penthouse?'

'Actually, I'm back at me mum's.'

Terry opened his door. 'That's great.'

'And Tel –' Justin began to run off down the street.

'Yeah?'

'It's the best thing you've ever done. *Ciao*.'

Joc Eldon wasn't pleased.

'Move it, super-star,' he told Steve Benson who was doing as little training as possible and was determined to do less. As trainer, there was not much love lost between him and Benson, largely because Benson was in his early thirties, had five England caps – and no chance of getting another. A dozen other players of the Third Division squad were training on the pitch, but none of them matched Benson's idleness. Even now he was skiving.

'It's the ankle.'

'You can walk to the bar,' said Eldon unsympathetically.

'Only if you're buying 'em, darling,' replied Benson condescendingly. Then he saw Justin hurrying over from the grandstand and, ignoring Eldon, Benson slouched over to meet him.

'Oi – this is supposed to be a training session.'

'Who told you that? I'll be back in a sec.'

'Who's this?' asked Eldon as Justin came into range. 'An agent for Real Madrid?'

Benson turned, treating Eldon to a cynical grin. 'No – he's my counsellor from Alcoholics Anonymous.'

'I'll give you three minutes.'

'Thanks, boss.'

Justin seemed surprised by Eldon's attitude and said so:

'You don't have to take that, do you?'

'I do.'

'But why?'

'Because I can't get into the First Team, that's why.'

'They can't even lace your boots.'

'Sure. Anyway – what's the score on your man?'

'Daley? We've got a meet.'

'You sure he's OK?' asked Benson, doubtfully.

'He's very big,' said Justin, reassuringly.

'I've never heard of him.'

'Maybe not. But he's a very well known man.'

'OK,' said Benson, his enthusiasm regained. 'I've got two thousand tickets for the England–Scotland match. Cash on the nail – face value – and you sell them for whatever you can get on the open market. And by the way –'

'Yeah?'

'You fix your own price.'

'Double, treble, even more, eh? Them Jocks – they'll rob banks to get football tickets.'

'That's why it's big,' said Benson. 'I could be a marked man for this. See – I've had a nice business with Little Phil. What I do is collect tickets from players in London – I mean, they always have tickets for the big games. But what do I get? Peanuts.'

'Little Phil takes you for granted.'

'You're right there.' Benson grinned. 'Why should I make him any richer? If I had the dough I'd buy the tickets meself. But I haven't. And you, my son, are potless.'

'Slightly embarrassed.'

'Skint.'

'Happens to us all.'

'Yeah. Anyway – I'm relying on you. I don't know any villains – you do.'

'I know 'em all,' said Justin proudly.

'Get me the best,' snapped Benson.

'Oi,' yelled Eldon. 'You still chewing the rag?'

The Jag nosed through the traffic whilst Terry took the brunt of one of Arthur's black moods.

'Terence – I don't *like* young people. So I certainly don't want to meet one of them.' Arthur drew on his cigar, cursing the traffic.

'He ain't "young people". He's a person – and he ain't a representative of the whole flaming generation, Arthur.'

'You seen 'em?'

They glanced through the window. 'There's one – and another. Both sexes, ain't they?'

'Don't come the jokester with me, Terence. They know it all, don't they? Slovenly, rude, opinionated.'

'This one reckons he's got Steve Benson in his pocket,' interrupted Terry.

'Old Benno?'

'Yeah – fair player.'

'Fair?' said Arthur wonderingly. 'He's brilliant. Even when he's had a few the night before, he can still pop the goals in.'

'That's right,' said Terry soothingly.

'And this – Justin. He's a pal of Benno's, is he?'

'You bet.'

'He's buying lunch?'

'He says so.'

'You sure he'll pay? I mean – I don't want to be put in an embarrassing situation. I'm a respectable businessman.'

'Yes, Arthur.'

'So – on your head be it, Terence.'

'Thanks, Arthur.'

He parked the car outside the restaurant and leant back for a moment in the driver's seat. 'You know something?'

'What?'

'You're taking the initiative, Terry. I'm not sure I like that.'

'We're talking about money, Arthur. Lots of it.'

'You take the initiative more often, then.' Arthur lit his cigar again and opened the door. 'I need money,' he said.

The interior of the Italian restaurant was smart, cool and inviting. As Arthur and Terry came in they saw Justin immediately, for he cut a distinctive appearance. He was wearing a light-weight suit, a good shirt and tie and there was a floppy handkerchief in his breast pocket. Justin, radiating confidence rose to his feet as Arthur trailed over to him, looking enigmatic.

'The great man. Don Daley, Numero Uno.' Justin took Arthur's hand and kissed it.

'Blimey.'

He hurried on, before Arthur could say anything else. 'You know what this is?'

'My –'

'This is one of the greatest days of my life.'

Terry winced in the background.

'No kidding. Sit. Sit.' He sounded a little as if he was talking to a dog. 'A glass of Soave, eh? How did I know you'd like Soave?'

Arthur shook his head bemusedly.

'I just knew.' Justin poured the wine and Terry grinned. He had never seen Arthur at such a loss for words.

'This is Justin – Arthur.'

'Pleased to meet you,' said Arthur weakly.

'He's sizing me up,' said Justin to Terry.

'Eh?'

'The old fox.' He squeezed Arthur's arm. 'I still can't believe it – me sitting with you, Arthur. Now – you don't mind me calling you Arthur, do you?'

'That's fine – Justin,' said Arthur in a voice of deep strain.

'I'll tell you what.' He continued to squeeze his arm.

'Yes?'

'In my book, you're a hero. I mean – you're up there with the stars. Bogie, Edward G, George Raft. Did you know him?'

'Who?' asked Arthur vacantly, but Terry could see that he was warming to the praise.

'George Raft – when he came to London.'

Arthur smiled modestly. He was beginning to enjoy himself. 'We had a few words.'

'I bet. I said to Terry – Terry, you're privileged to work with Arthur Daley.'

'When was that?' asked Terry cynically.

'Told you dozens of times,' continued Justin, quite unabashed.

'Now, Arthur –'

'Yes, Justin.'

'You can help me.'

'I can?' For a moment Arthur looked a little suspicious. Then he succumbed to Justin's charm as the talk swept over him.

'You've got it all – knowledge, experience, wisdom.'

'Well –'

'I'm just climbing the ladder, a mere apprentice. It's like Leonardo da Vinci – he had the idea, grand design and then he had all those wallies, apprentices, I mean, putting in a nose or a tree or a bit of sky. They were learning, weren't they? Learning from the master. And that's why I'm grateful to break bread with you, Arthur.'

'Talking about bread,' said Terry, breaking into the sycophantic chat. 'Any chance of seeing the menu?' But he could see that Arthur was purring.

'Sorry, Tel,' said Justin. 'I was getting carried away.' He waved at the Head Waiter. 'Mario.'

Terry looked at Arthur. He seemed swathed in a reverie. Then he caught Terry's eye and sighed. 'You don't understand ambition, Terence. This young man is right.'

'Oh, yeah?'

'The kind of advice that I can give him is rather special. You don't get it in college.'

Mario appeared and much to Terry's relief, he was brandishing menus. '*Signorini.*'

'Mario,' said Justin, 'I want you to meet Mister Daley. Mister Arthur Daley. He is a man of respect – is that the expression?'

'It is the expression.' He bowed low to Arthur. 'I am delighted to meet you. Many people talk about you.'

Arthur straightened his tie and beamed. 'Do they?'

'Arthur Daley,' continued Mario, 'I would rather have you in my restaurant than Egon Ronay. Please – enjoy yourself.'

He's a pro if nothing else, thought Terry as Mario left the menus and hurried on to greet another customer in different, but somehow similar effusive tones.

'What a nice man,' said Arthur.

'Mario's great.' Justin's enthusiasm was making Terry tired again.

'Just as well.' Terry wanted to put the boot in – anything to break up the sickly enclave. 'His partner was after you a year ago. Remember?'

Arthur looked at him glazedly.

'You sold a Merc to him.'

'Who?'

'What's his name? Angelo? The one who sent a solicitor's letter to you.'

Arthur sighed and then smiled at Terry patronisingly. 'As usual, you've got it all wrong. Thaz man had a little caff in the Harrow Road. How did *I* know it was stolen?' Arthur looked injured. 'Even the judge said I was a pawn in the game.'

'Yeah,' replied Terry. 'Pity the jury decided you was a lobster.'

'I still got away with a three hundred pound fine, didn't I?'

Arthur looked guardedly at Justin, wishing he had not admitted to that.

Justin squeezed his wrist again, this time very excitedly and Arthur drew back in pain. 'That's what I was saying to you, Arthur.'

'What?'

'How you can help me. After all, you know all the dodges.'

'I'm not sure that –'

'In fact you're an utter, thorough, unmitigated *rogue*.'

'I beg your pardon?'

'That's why I admire you.'

Arthur smiled sweetly at the dubious compliment.

'You've got him in one,' said Terry.

A pained smile crossed Arthur's face as he looked down the menu. 'I think I'll have the spaghetti bolognaise,' he said reflectively. 'Now,' he began in a business-like tone, turning to Justin. 'I gather you have an offer that I may have to reject.'

Meanwhile, down at the football ground, Little Phil sat beside the driver of his Cadillac. They drove into the car-park and he got out, standing grandly by his car in an enormous astrakhan coat that seemed to swamp his tiny body.

'Hey!' Little Phil spotted Benson walking towards his Sierra. He looked up unwillingly and then slowly began to walk towards him. Little Phil treated him to a cold smile.

'Suddenly I don't hear from you?'

'I've been busy.'

'Busy? You don't even play.'

'Now look –'

'I don't even see your name in the papers anymore. We had a meet last week and you didn't show. What's up? I've been generous to you, Benno.'

'You kidding? I get buttons.'

Little Phil poked a stubby finger into Benson's chest. 'Most people don't want to know about you.'

'I see.'

'But I'm a sentimentalist. I remember you when you was a fine player.'

'How would you know?' said Benson with a sneer.

'Don't get clever with me, pal.' Little Phil was gradually losing his temper. 'We need to have a serious discussion.'

'What about?'

'The tartan army – what else?'

'I'm having negotiations with other people,' snapped Benson.

'You what?'

'You heard.'

'There *are* no other people. If people want briefs for Wimbledon they come to me. Don't give me all that stuff about other people.'

'They're well connected,' said Benson uneasily.

'With who?'

'Top men. Kings of the underworld.' He was defensive now.

'You mean they gotta sauna club in Upper Norwood?'

'They got muscle.'

'See Cedric over there?' said Phil menacingly, pointing out his burly driver. 'You want to know about muscle? And there's a hundred more where he came from. You tell your friends that.'

Justin poured more wine.

'You see – old Benno's got this friend who works in the office at Wembley Stadium. Now this friend –' He paused to see Arthur hanging on his every word and even Terry was beginning to look interested. 'He can get two thousand tickets for the England–Scotland game.'

'Nicked, you mean,' said Arthur knowingly.

'No.'

Arthur looked at him in surprise.

'He's got to settle the books. You know people have to apply by post to get the tickets, right? What's more, you have to live in England to stop all the Scotties from flooding the sacred turf. I mean – the Jocks are going to appeal to the Race Relations Board. Well, what he does is this – he ignores some of the letters. That's the beauty of it, see, he ignores 'em. Then he keeps two thousand tickets to his self. It's legal – they don't care as long as they get the dough. And I said to Benno – there's only one man who can handle this – Arthur Daley. He's got the contacts, the muscle, the organisation. And sod Little Phil.'

'Er – how much?' asked Arthur tentatively.

Justin smiled at Terry. 'No messing about with the Guv'nor, eh?' He turned back to Arthur respectfully. 'Sixteen grand for two thousand, eight pound seats, plus a drink for him, say two grand. We're talking, Arthur, about eighteen grand.'

Arthur stared at him with spaghetti dribbling down his chin. 'How much?'

'Eighteen –'

'Yeah,' said Arthur sadly. 'I heard it.'

Terry gave a wry grin. 'I'd like to hear that again,' he said, happily conscious of Arthur scowling at him.

'You'd treble that in a week,' said Justin. 'Even more.'

Arthur spoke slowly and carefully. 'Let's get this straight – you want *me* to lend *you* eighteen grand.'

'Not lend – it's an investment.'

'Is it now?' Arthur looked devastated.

'We'll split the profit – obviously you'll get the lion's share.'

'Thank you.'

'I thought you'd grab the idea.' Justin's enthusiasm was undiminished by the parchment grey hue of Arthur's face. 'It's like printing money, innit?'

'Ah,' said Arthur leaning back in his chair, 'the impetuosity of youth.' He turned to Terry, gave a sad smile and then addressed himself to Justin again. 'You want to know about wisdom, Justin?'

'From your lips.'

'Then let me give you this advice – first sus it out. If someone offers you a bargain – there *has* to be a catch in it.'

'Not in this one. Honest,' reassured Justin.

'That's the catch.'

'Eh?' For the first time Justin was thrown.

'When I hear the word honest,' said Arthur, 'I reach for my solicitor.'

'You've got to trust me.'

'Why?'

Justin considered for a second. 'You're right – who needs trust? I'm being very naive.'

'You are, my man, you are.' Arthur was censorious and patronising all at the same time.

Justin treated him to an eager smile. 'I'm learning. Now I've got two thousand tickets for a football game.' He paused. 'Got any contacts in Scotland?'

'Naturally,' said Arthur grandly.

'I mean – big contacts.'

Arthur turned to Terry and said commandingly, 'Tell him.'

'What?' Terry gazed at Arthur uncomprehendingly.

'Tell him about Big Hamish.'

'Oh him.'

'Well –' encouraged Arthur.

'Yeah,' Terry hesitated. 'He's big – 'bout five foot ten. He's violent. He's –'

'Never mind,' said Arthur hurriedly returning his attention to Justin. 'He's a personal friend of mine, is Hamish – the top man, chairman of the board. Know what I mean?'

'Phone him.'

'Eh?' Arthur looked as if the pace was getting too much for him.

'Phone him. Mario.' Justin beckoned back to the head waiter. 'Show the gentleman where the phone is.'

'At once, *Signori*.'

'He's learning,' said Arthur to Terry as he rose majestically to his feet. 'Learning fast.'

Little Phil was sitting in the big back seat of the Cadillac, in a pensive mood, while Cedric drove him through the traffic.

'You try to help,' he said. 'You really try.'

'You always help people, Phil,' said Cedric supportively. 'You don't get credit for your charity work either.'

'True. People don't know about that, do they?'

'That's because you're an anonymous benefactor, Phil.'

'I don't get any recognition for it, do I?'

'You should get an OBE.'

'It's orphans and widows,' muttered Little Phil, 'and bloody dishonest footballers. Who's Benno's pal, then?'

'Oh, 'im.'

'Who's 'im?'

'Justin something. Right ice-cream.'

'He is, is he?'

'Flash git – no form.'

'Never mind,' said Little Phil and was silent for a while.

Eventually Cedric asked him:

'Something you'd like to tell me, boss?'

'Something I'd like you to do.'

'Say the word –'

'Why don't you give this flash Justin a pull?'

Arthur returned from the telephone, gracefully thanking Mario as he passed him.

'My pleasure, Signor Daley.'

'Incidentally – I've always had a passion for Italian merchandise.'

'Yes, *Signor*?'

'There's an item in one of my warehouses.'

Mario immediately looked cagey.

'An espresso machine.'

'They are very good –'

'Almost brand new, this one,' confided Arthur. 'The same model they use in the snack-bar in the Vatican.'

Mario looked at him, suddenly dazed. 'The Vatican?'

Arthur gave him a virtuous smile. 'So they say. Mark you, I'm not suggesting that it's been sanctified.'

'I'm pleased to hear that.'

'But, if you're interested –' Arthur began to walk back to the table.

Mario put a restraining hand on his arm and whispered, 'Signor Daley –'

'Yes?'

'How much?'

'Well, now.' Arthur passed him a visiting card. 'Someone's always there. Do drop in.'

Justin anxiously gazed at Arthur as he arrived back at the table. 'What gives, Arthur?'

Nonchalantly, Arthur sat down and picked up his glass. 'Nice drop of wine, that.'

'Hamish?' asked Justin, anxiously pouring out more.

'Oh yeah – Hamish,' said Arthur ruminatively. 'He was having his mince and toddies, wasn't he?'

'Was he?' asked Terry innocently.

'And when he's done his rhubarb and custard you know what he'll do?'

'What's that?' Justin was hanging on Arthur's every word.

'He'll jump on an inter-city.'

Later that evening, Arthur, Terry and Justin were waiting at Euston Station for the Glasgow Express to arrive at platform twelve. Arthur was saying to Justin: 'You'll like Hamish – bit of a rough diamond, but his heart's in the right place. And he doesn't have too much rabbit – yes Justin?'

'You're the Guv'nor,' said Justin. 'Like a teacher to me.'

'You booked him a hotel?' Terry's voice had a sudden suspicious note to it.

'Not really,' said Arthur innocently.

'So?'

'I thought he could kip at your drum.'

Terry remained silent, watching the train draw in.

'OK?' asked Arthur hopefully.

'No.'

'Terence – he's a colleague.'

'He growls.'

'What?'

'I said, he growls.' Terry was scanning the arriving passengers now. 'Then he attacks. I had three fights when he came here last year.'

'Just high spirits,' said Arthur dismissively.

'Yeah – Teachers, Bells, Chivas Regal and any other spirits he can get hold of.'

'I've never heard him growl,' said Arthur.

'You don't listen, do you?'

'This him?' asked Justin, nudging Arthur.

'No.'

'He looks like a growler – big bloke.'

'That's not him. Where the hell is he?' Arthur was beginning to look worried. Then a large gentleman, smartly dressed with an overnight bag, glasses and a nasty scar down his cheek, walked over to Arthur and said:

'Mister Daley?'

'Eh?' Arthur took a step back, temporarily thrown and instinctively exhibiting his timid nature.

'My name's Alisdair.'

'Oh yeah?'

'He's not coming.'

'What?'

Alisdair looked round furtively. 'I must ask you not to shout.'

'Who are you?' Arthur hissed.

'I've just told you.'

'Where is he?'

'I've just told you.' He looked helplessly at Terry and Justin. 'Is he a cretin or something?'

Terry was just about to reply, when Arthur said: 'What are you doing here?'

'I'm Hamish's proxy.'

'Who?'

'His stand-in. Hamish is in hospital.'

'What's he picked up?'

'Two broken legs, broken wrist, dislocated shoulder, multiple cuts and abrasions.'

'Street accident?'

'Aye,' said Alisdair quickly, 'It was in the street.' He nodded at Terry and Justin. 'This the gang?'

Grudgingly, still thinking about Hamish's mysterious street accident, Arthur introduced them. Alisdair turned back to Arthur. 'Hamish said that you were a good man to do business with.'

Arthur bridled, while Justin said, 'Numero Uno.'

'You what?' asked Alisdair suspiciously.

'You're talking to the top man. Arthur's met them all – George Raft, Murder Incorporated. He's nation-wide, coast to coast. You ain't talking to some little Gorbals tearaway, you know.'

Alisdair gave Justin a strong stare. 'Who is he?'

'He's with me,' said Terry.

Alisdair treated them to a frosty smile. 'Just before Hamish lapsed into unconsciousness –'

'Poor chap,' said Arthur respectfully.

'– he muttered something about tickets. He didn't say anything about a hotel room.'

Arthur gave Terry a pointed glare. 'Hamish usually made his own arrangements.'

'Fine,' said Alisdair, 'so have I.'

'Oh yes?'

'I've booked at the Hilton.' He began to walk towards the exit. 'I expect you know the way, Mr Daley.' Arthur followed him as if mesmerised.

'I'll tell you one thing, Arthur,' said Terry.

'What's that?' asked Arthur, feebly.

'He don't growl, does he?'

Terry sat in the front passenger seat of Arthur's Jag, while Justin stretched out in the rear. They were parked outside the Hilton.

'Ain't we on the firm?' asked Justin a little plaintively.

'No.'

'Why not, Terry?'

'It's high finance time now, innit?'

'Yeah – but is he going to stitch us up?' Justin sounded restless, insecure.

'Who's us?'

'Me and Benno. I mean – is the great man honest?'

'No.'

Justin suddenly sat up. 'Now you tell me.'

'Work it out for yourself.'

'I'm learning, Terry.'

'Well – let the Deputy Head take over. Are you paying attention, Justin?'

'I'm all ears.'

'Arthur's been around for a long time and he knows the worth of a pound. Know what I mean?'

'No.'

'Anyway – what's your problem? Yesterday you had nothing and tomorrow you *may* have a few bob. That's fair enough, innit?'

Justin spoke reluctantly. 'I s'pose so.'

'Don't worry about Arthur,' Terry said matily. 'It's the other guy you should be worrying about.'

Inside Alisdair's luxury hotel room, all was quiet, all was calm as the high level negotiations took place. Alisdair, with his suit jacket draped over a chair, was tucking into room service, whilst Arthur, too mean to add to the bill, watched him reflectively.

'That's a bit steep, Arthur, isn't it?'

'Is it, Alisdair?' Arthur's voice was warm, friendly.

'Thirty-five grand?' He did a quick calculation. 'That's about seventeen pounds fifty pence per ticket.'

'That's about right,' said Arthur cheerfully.

'It's steep. My people won't like that.'

'You still have a handy profit. Some of the Jocks would commit murder for a ticket. Present company excepted, of course,' added Arthur hastily.

'Aye,' said Alisdair after a meaningful pause. 'I reckon they would.'

Arthur, still anxious to appease a social gaff, said: 'A figure of speech.'

'No.'

'Eh?'

'You got it right first time.'

'They love their football,' said Arthur enthusiastically.

'Now wait a minute. Just for a second – let's forget the tickets. I just want you to think about the logistics, Arthur. Yes?' Alisdair flung his napkin down on the table and began to pace around. 'Shall we say – ten – no, twenty thousand punters are converging on Wembley from Scotland.'

'Why not?' said Arthur, trying to get comfortable.

'Now, let's assume each punter has got one hundred pounds in his pocket – and that would be a liberal assessment.'

'Quite.' Arthur cleared his throat.

'I see an army on the move.' Alisdair's eyes were very bright as he continued to pace up and down. 'One hundred pounds times ten thousand equals one million pounds.' He stood back in awe of his own calculations. 'A million, Arthur – I'm giving you a million. All of it.'

'Very generous, Alisdair.'

'All you have to do is to get the money out of their pockets. Look man – from the moment they cross the border they're fair game. They have to be fed, sheltered – and more importantly – refreshed.' He paused and turned to Arthur with near religious zeal. 'It's a remarkable prospect, is it not?'

'A remarkable prospect indeed.' Arthur echoed the words with awe and with greed.

Alisdair smiled and said, 'Want topping up, Arthur?'

Arthur stared at his glass, still thinking of the prospect. 'I could handle a drop,' he said.

Alisdair poured him another glass of champagne. Then he spoke slowly, confidently. 'Tickets are a mere bagatelle. A drop in the limitless ocean. What I am suggesting is a huge exercise, a major operation.' He leant forward confidently.

'You see, Arthur – you have to realise that the world is ruled by accountants now and,' he added hastily, 'a few entrepreneurs like yourself.'

'I assume I'm talking to an accountant?' said Arthur with a quick smirk.

'You've got it in one, Arthur,' Alisdair replied. 'We want to get together an attractive package. Say – two nights in London, decent bed, continental breakfast, a couple of hand-picked clubs and a ticket for the game.' He paused to consider the deal. 'People will pawn their videos to get to Wembley. It'll be a weekend of a lifetime.'

'I like it,' replied Arthur. 'I like it. Incidentally, a pal of mine has three thousand autographed photos of Charlie Nicholas. They'd make a nice souvenir, wouldn't they?'

Alisdair gave him a mirthless grin. 'Why not, Arthur. You're the kind of guy we need. You know this city. We can guarantee the bodies, but it's up to you to bury them.'

'You're suggesting a partnership?'

'That's it. Mind you, I still have to meet other people.'

'Like who?' asked Arthur with instant suspicion.

'Do you know a man called Phil?'

'Oh yeah. He's a very good man if you want to go to the Royal Ballet.' Arthur tried to look casual. 'But if you want briefs for England and Scotland – I'm your man.'

'We've worked with him before,' said Alisdair doubtfully. 'He reckons he can get any amount of tickets . . .'

'Does he?'

'Aye.'

'He's a dreamer,' commented Arthur patronisingly, 'old Phil. He doesn't realise that I've taken over –'

'I like your confidence, Arthur.' He paused and then leant forward again, this time with the kind of directness that made Arthur wary. 'Are you ready to go to Glasgow?'

'Well –'

'Put the tickets on the table, meet my associates and shake hands?'

'There's a few details I have to settle first.' Arthur shifted uneasily and took a long draft of champagne.

'In principle, I mean?'

'Oh yeah . . . in principle. And Glasgow very soon,' said Arthur, 'very, very soon.'

'Maybe tomorrow?' asked Alisdair.

'Glasgow, eh?' Arthur gave a glum smile.

'The natives are really quite friendly.'

'Who said?' asked Arthur uncertainly.

Terry watched Arthur leave the hotel. For a moment he stood by the kerb, preoccupied, chewing at his cigar. Then he ambled slowly round the corner, as if he were sleep-walking.

'Now what's he doing?' asked Terry rhetorically. He opened the door and bellowed: 'Oi, we're over here!'

But there was no reaction from Arthur as he turned the corner. Cursing, Terry got out of the car and walked briskly after him.

'Arthur – where you going?' he said when he finally caught up with him.

Arthur continued to walk slowly, reflectively, along the street. 'I'm thinking – you know, oiling the old grey matter, considering things.'

'You can do that in the motor.'

'With young Justin committing GBH of the Donalds?'

'I've never seen you thinking, Arthur,' said Terry wonderingly.

'You may scoff, but this is a command decision. Have you ever dipped into your pocket and come out with eighteen grand? Course not,' he said before Terry could answer. 'It's beyond your experience, innit?'

'Well – I've had a pull from the Inland Revenue.'

'What's that – two bob?' asked Arthur sneeringly. 'They probably owe you. I'm talking about *real* money.'

'Have you got real money?'

'Course I have. That's not the point. My dough's tied up.'

'Can't you get it from your bank?'

'Oh yeah,' said Arthur with withering sarcasm. 'How about this for starters. Please mister bank manager – I've got two thousand hooky football tickets.' He paused expectantly, looking at Terry questioningly. 'I mean, it ain't exactly an extension for the kitchen or a new roof. Anyway, I'm borrowing me own dough. I've got to sell the tickets. You've got to realise, we're into a high risk venture, Terry. What happens if Alisdair's pals don't want to buy?' Arthur's eyes dilated with horror at the thought. Then he continued looking glazed. 'Or maybe they do, but we get hi-jacked on the way back to London.' He plucked at Terry's sleeve. 'All kinds of things can happen. An earthquake? What happened to Hamish the Growler? Who knows? So that's why I'm schlepping around the environs of Park Lane and thinking, and thinking, and thinking. Can't you understand, Terence, I'm thinking. So just leave me alone.'

Arthur turned away abruptly and walked down the street, leaving Terry calling after him. 'Should we wait?'

'Obviously,' said Arthur impatiently. 'I'm not going to think all night, am I?'

Cedric lumbered up the stairs of the council block. Once he had reached the scruffy, graffiti-strewn landing he began to look for a number. Eventually he found it, but before he could knock, the door opened. A woman stood there, looking harassed. She was in her early forties and still bore some vestiges of tarnished glamour.

'Who are you?' she asked brusquely.

Cedric gave her what he hoped was a winning smile. 'Justin about?'

'You police?' she asked.

'Not me, love. I'm a friend of Justin's – me and Steve Benson.'

She turned and shouted into the flat. 'Justin – it's for you.' She returned her jaundiced gaze to Cedric. 'I'm late for work – I hope he's heard me.'

'Don't you worry, Mrs James,' said Cedric reassuringly, 'I'll give him a yell.'

'Could you? I'll miss my bus. Ta-ra.' She walked quickly to the staircase and Cedric walked into the flat.

Glancing into the living-room, he saw no one, but along

the hall was a closed door. Cedric opened the door to find Justin in bed, sleeping peacefully. With sudden dexterity Cedric grabbed the mattress and pitched Justin on to the floor.

'All you ponces lie in bed all day. Look at you with your mum going out to work and all.'

Justin grabbed at the bedclothes, blinking in the hard light of day.

'Who are you?' he asked blearily.

'Who am I? I get up early in the morning and then I hit people.'

Justin stared at him unbelievingly and Cedric continued with his disarming explanation.

'I work for Phil,' he said. 'I bet you don't work?'

'I'm self-employed,' replied Justin trying to gather up his ruffled composure – and pyjamas.

'What as? A thief?' Cedric asked unpleasantly. Then he came up very close to the still sprawling Justin and stood over him menacingly. 'You're thieving my livelihood.'

'What?'

'I mean, Benno tells me that you're a go-between and you know the missing link. Who is he?'

'Ask Benno,' said Justin feebly.

'He doesn't know him.'

Justin draped the bedclothes over his shoulders. '*Numero Uno*.' He stated.

'Who's he?'

'The man who's going to slaughter you and your gu'nor.'

Cedric thought about that statement for a while. Then said quietly, 'What I'm going to do is smother you with your duvet. Fancy that?'

Justin stared at him, wondering just how serious he was. 'If I tell you, you'll be out of here in two seconds?'

'Try me.'

'Arthur Daley.' Justin spoke with great confidence and a long pause ensued. Then Cedric repeated with a grin:

'Arthur Daley?'

'Yeah. I thought you'd be worried.'

But Cedric didn't seem worried at all. Instead he giggled, even guffawed. Justin looked disturbed for this was a far cry from the reaction he had hoped for.

'Dear oh dear,' said Cedric, tears running down his cheeks. 'I think I'm going to wet meself.'

'You wouldn't say that to him?'

'Why not?'

'Well, you wouldn't.'

'I would. Him and his punch-drunk pal and his relatives and his creditors who are many, and his debtors, who are few – the whole bunch of 'em.' Cedric began to laugh again and, to Justin, it was not a pleasant sound.

'Yeah?' asked Justin, his confidence draining.

'Oh yeah,' said Cedric, squatting down beside him on the floor. 'So why don't you tell me all about it?'

Theo Warren was bald, fifty, confident and friendly. He sat behind his executive desk as if it fitted him – as if it was part of him. Sitting uneasily opposite him was Arthur, staring at a chart on the wall which was covered by zigzag lines and numbers.

'What's all that about, Theo?'

'It's a graph – assets, capital, deposits – it's to encourage the customers.'

'Yeah, but what does it mean?'

'I don't know. It looks good, doesn't it?'

'It's brilliant.' He grew silent. 'I went to your other place, the bank.'

'Not anymore. I only run a bank for a year, Arthur – otherwise the Fraud Squad get busy. It's a time-share property company now. You don't want an apartment in a baronial castle in Wales, do you?'

'Whereabouts?' said Arthur chattily.

'We don't know yet. Now I hope you don't want a mortgage, Arthur.'

Arthur, not to be hurried, looked around him. 'This outfit a good earner?'

'Good? I tell you what – it's going so well I'm thinking of

turning it into an honest business.'

'Never!'

'No, never. You see – and you know this yourself – there are those who take and there are those who are taken. It's all greed.' He winked at Arthur and then gazed at him affectionately. 'We offer a nice rate of interest and we're competitive. And we're the leaders in the field. Now, if the other societies put up their rates it would be to the good of the public, wouldn't it?'

'Yeah, I suppose so. But you don't pay out.'

'That's a different thing, Arthur. I'm talking about the principle. We offer good value.'

'So I believe.' He glanced around him more warily now. 'Er, I understand you're financing some – projects?'

'Money's the game, Arthur.' Theo whispered.

'Of course.'

'My lips are sealed. But try this: four characters who didn't have two bob between them put up a scheme. Have you got any collateral, I asked them. A safe vault, they said. You couldn't get any better collateral than that, could you? They wanted twelve grand for the laser welding equipment and the protective clothing. A first class investment, I thought. And as it was I got it back in three weeks. So what's your problem, Arthur?'

Arthur looked taken aback. 'I'm not a robber, you know,' he began to protest.

'Some say yes, some say no.'

Arthur ignored him. 'I'm a simple general dealer and I need eighteen grand for two or three days.'

'What for?' Theo asked solicitously.

'Do you trust me?'

'No.'

Arthur frowned and tried again. 'I've got tickets. Wembley. For the England–Scotland do. What I don't need is any welding equipment.'

Theo considered for a moment and then said abruptly, 'OK. Three and a quarter per cent per day.'

Arthur began to do complicated calculations on his

fingers. 'That's five hundred and eighty-five quid.'

'Give us a chance, Arthur,' Theo protested. 'I haven't even got me calculator yet.'

'The figures are OK – don't you worry about that,' said Arthur reassuringly. 'If I need it for a week you're copping twenty-two and three-quarters per cent interest.'

'Why don't you go down to the Woolwich?' Theo checked on his pocket calculator.

'I think it's diabolical,' said Arthur.

'It depends on what side of the desk you're on. You're good at sums, Arthur.'

'Five per cent for three days, eh?'

'That's a bit strong, Arthur.'

'Well, I'm not going to knock you, am I?' Arthur's tone was all injured innocence.

'Never been known. One way or another we always get paid.'

Arthur looked at him in surprise. 'Theo! We're friends!'

Theo shook his head.

'Come on,' said Arthur, but Theo still shook his head.

'We're acquaintances. Three per cent for forty-eight hours. And then three and a quarter per day.'

'Yeah, OK.' Arthur sounded defeated.

Theo rose triumphantly and took his cheque book from a drawer. 'We'll have to go to my bank.'

'Haven't you got cash here?'

'You must be kidding. The villains who come into this place?'

Arthur smiled sadly. 'That's the world,' he said. 'It's a wicked place.'

Another business conference was taking place in a different part of town, but this one was a little more formal. There was no friendship here – merely the Income Tax Inspector and Terry, gripped by mutual interest.

'You missed the tea-lady, Mr McCann. You don't mind if I drink my coffee?'

'Sure – go ahead.'

'You do understand that this is not an investigation? I'm only trying to elicit information. The thing is –' He hesitated. 'We seem to have lost track of you, Mr McCann.'

'Really?'

'How would you describe your occupation?'

'Tricky, innit? Just odds and ends.'

'Self-employed?' he asked blandly.

'I just get by.' The reply was casual.

'Freelance?'

'I dunno.'

'What I'm trying to get at is your income – haphazard as it may be.'

'That's the word,' said Terry frankly. 'It's so haphazard that I don't know what it is.'

The income tax inspector gave a patient, resigned smile. 'Should I try another tack? Have you a PAYE code number?'

'What's that?'

'Precisely. We'll ignore that then.' He was beginning to look tired and pressed a button on his desk. 'Unemployment benefit?'

Terry shook his head.

'Social security supplementary benefit?'

Terry shook his head again.

'You don't contribute to national insurance? Or, as we used to call it – stamping your cards?'

Terry shook his head yet again, but the Inspector was determined to be thorough.

'Mortgage, HP? Credit cards? Pension fund?'

'None of them,' said Terry.

The Inspector stared at the desk-top and picked up his pipe, filling it thoughtfully with tobacco.

'You've cracked it, haven't you?' he muttered.

'Beg your pardon?'

'The system. You haven't got a number. You're not a statistic. You're a spirit – a spectre. They hardly know about you. Where were you when they did the census?'

'I was out.'

'I bet you were.' He gazed at Terry as if he was an entirely new species – unrecorded man.

The door opened and an attractive young woman entered, carrying a file and some letters. She put them down on the desk.

'Thank you, Miss Demosthenous,' said the inspector, smirking at her.

Terry was spellbound, for Miss Demosthenous had, without doubt, the best legs in London. As she made a graceful exit, the inspector lit his pipe and glanced at Terry.

'They're amazing, aren't they? The best legs in the Department of Inland Revenue and she's not a bad typist either.'

'Fantastic,' said Terry.

The Inspector paused, his mind reluctantly reverting to other matters. 'You know what you are, Mr McCann? You're the invisible man. Where's your identity? What happens if we have a war? You'll dodge it, won't you? We've been after you for seven years and during that period you must have had some job – just some job.' He sounded as if he was beginning to plead.

Terry thought, then he said, 'Well, last week, for example, I was minding a pub for two nights because they thought there might be some bovver. I got fifteen pounds in cash for each night, plus a drink and a couple of sandwiches. I don't need an account for that, do I?'

'What are you saying?' The inspector looked wild-eyed. 'Are you some kind of itinerant bodyguard?'

'I'm an odd job man.'

The Inspector exhaled a whiff of tobacco and picked up the file left by the exquisite Miss Demosthenous.

'Daley,' he said and Terry winced at the all too familiar name.

'Does that mean anything?'

'Who did you say?' he asked despondently.

'Mister Daley – are you his gardener?'

'His what?' he gaped at the Inspector, unable to take in this latest gambit.

'Gardener – as in Percy Thrower.'

'He hasn't got a bloody garden.'

The inspector's eyes gleamed. 'Hasn't he now?'

Terry made a quick recovery, realising that he had made a mistake. 'Mind you, he's got a big balcony and he does like a daffodil and a, er, Busy Lizzie. Actually, he's well into horticultural affairs.'

The Inspector gave Terry a manic grin. 'Minding the flowers, eh?'

'You've got it. How much do I get?'

He looked down at his file. 'Let's have a look. Oh, yes. The financial year April 1982. Fifteen hundred pounds. That's more-or-less thirty pounds a week. It's creeping up, isn't it? What with the occasional stint at a boozer, any other odds and ends and suddenly you're liable to pay tax.'

Terry sat there in gloomy silence.

'Unless you wish to state that Mr Daley is falsifying his claim and his books?'

'Mr Daley wouldn't dream of doing that – he's as honest as the day.'

'You don't do any other gardens?' asked the Inspector eagerly.

'No,' said Terry. 'I'm not into digging up the earth. I'm a speciality man – balconies only. Of course, at a stretch I'd do a window box, as well.'

'That's nice to know,' said the inspector, busily making notes.

An impatient Arthur drummed his fingers on the pub counter. He kept glancing at his watch and sighing, showing all the symptoms of a busy man who was deeply frustrated by time being wasted. So when at last he saw Terry entering, Arthur's mood was sour.

'Long enough, weren't you?'

'Was I?'

'This is a big day for me. I've just put my life on the line.'

'Not on the clothes-line in the garden by any chance? Is there a drink going?'

'No – we're on a tight schedule.'

'Oh yeah?' Then he began to chant, 'Arthur Daley, quite contrary, How does your garden grow?' Terry paused and said angrily, 'You owe me fifteen hundred sovs.'

Arthur drained his glass. 'What're you talking about?' he asked innocently.

'The trusty old retainer.'

'Who?'

'Me.'

'I don't understand, Terence.'

'The one with manure on his wellies – the gardener. You've been just a bit too clever this time, Arthur. You're sussed.'

'You didn't grass on me, did you?' asked Arthur worriedly.

'No, I didn't. And you haven't got any in your bleeding garden either.'

'Now, Terry –'

'Listen, Arthur,' said Terry bitterly. 'You dropped me right up to the neck in your compost and you'll get away with it. But I won't, 'cos I'm going to be assessed now.'

'You don't understand –'

'I understand fifteen hundred sovs.'

'You'll get a drink out of it.'

'What? A watering-canful?'

Together, in uneasy companionship, Terry and Arthur walked towards the door of the pub.

'It's more important,' said Arthur.

'What is?'

'That I'm solvent.'

'Who says?'

'Me. I'm the brains of this organisation, you know.'

'Hang on.'

'Eh?'

The beautiful Miss Demosthenous had just entered the pub by another door and Terry had swung round to feast his eyes on her legs. 'Fantastic.'

'What?'

'Those legs – she should get the Nobel Prize.'

Arthur sighed a world-weary sigh. 'Terence. We're talking about serious things and you're rabbiting on about legs. Is that the only topic that exercises your mind? No wonder you're at the bottom of the heap. Handyman and occasional gardener . . . dear oh dear . . . you've got to do better than that.'

'Arthur,' said Terry patiently.

'Yeah?'

'Shut it.'

The Jag was crowded. Arthur drove, Terry sat beside him and Justin and Benson were in the back.

Arthur glanced back at Benson and said, 'Old memories, eh, Benno?'

Through the windows they could see the twin towers of Wembley Stadium in the distance.'

'Yeah.'

'I was always a great fan of yours,' said Arthur nostalgically. 'Why Greenwood didn't use you more I could never understand.'

'Bit of an expert are you, eh?' Benson said in a surly voice.

But Arthur was oblivious. 'As a matter of fact, I know 'em all – Mooro, Greavesie, Banksie, Ballie, Bestie, Webbo, Robbo, Stroller, Chopper and Sniffer – I know 'em all.'

'And Groucho and Harpo,' put in Terry helpfully.

'Who did they play for – Orient?'

'Odeon, wasn't it?'

Suddenly Arthur caught hold of the joke. He didn't like it. 'A bit of a jester, eh?' he said sourly. 'Well now, where do we meet the man with the tickets?'

'In his office. You give me the money and I give it to him. I'm in and out in three minutes,' said Benson.

'I don't even meet him?'

'He's worried –'

'*He's* worried –' Arthur stared at Benson in the mirror but it was not direct enough so he turned round in his seat, unconcerned about the road. 'I've got to give you the eighteen grand in cold blood and –'

Terry started as a pedestrian brushed the car. 'Arthur – you almost killed someone,' he pointed out.

'So what?' snarled Arthur. 'What's more important – life or money?'

With that little homily, he drove into the vast, almost empty car-park of Wembley Stadium, steering the Jag towards the entrance steps. They all got out of the car, but Arthur beckoned Terry and walked away from the other two leaving Justin and Benson to watch them suspiciously. Arthur took an envelope from his inside pocket and gave it furtively to Terry.

'Eighteen grand – I'm trusting you.'

'Do you think I'm going to do a runner?'

'Who knows? With that kind of dough. No – I'm talking about Benson. I mean, he was a very elusive player, wasn't he? A bit quick in the box and very greedy, as well. So, listen – you give him the dough and you wait for three minutes. If he don't appear you break doors, windows and shout and scream.'

Terry looked bewildered. 'He's got to talk to the man, hasn't he? Three minutes isn't enough, Arthur,' he protested.

'All right, four.'

'Five minutes at least. Maybe he wants a cup of tea.'

Arthur looked at him in amazement. 'Why?'

'Well – people do *have* a cup of tea, you know.'

'You sound like somebody in a war film.'

'You make everybody nervous – that's the trouble with you, Arthur.'

He took the envelope from Arthur who watched him handle it apprehensively. 'Don't drop it!'

'That's what I mean –' said Terry. He walked up to Benson and together they climbed the steps to the entrance, watched by an all too anxious Arthur.

Terry and Benson's footsteps echoed as they tramped down the wide, desolate corridor, usually thronged with people on match days, that skirted the stadium. Benson pointed to a staircase.

'It's up there,' he said pointing out a door marked OFFICE at the top of the stairs.

Terry glanced around before giving the envelope to Benson. 'Arthur's a bit worried about you.'

'Where can I hide?' said Benson reassuringly. He stuffed the envelope in his pocket and grinned. 'Be fair. We're all on the same side,' he said and ran up the staircase.

Terry moved over to a point where he could see the pitch and gazed down on its empty desolation. Then he glanced up at the vaulted ceiling, suddenly finding everything very oppressive.

Meanwhile, Arthur was prowling around the Jag, chewing his cigar. Justin was ready with his pupil/master relationship well to the fore.

'You've probably done things like this before, haven't you, Arthur?'

Arthur made an effort at coolness. 'All the time.'

'What was it like in the war?'

'You mean the fighting and everything?'

'No. I mean all the dodges – petrol, clothing coupons and things. What about chocolate?'

'I was doing my bit. Six gallons of petrol and you could live like a king. A dozen bars of fruit and nut and you thought you'd done something against the Hun. Mind you – it was tough.'

'I bet.'

'You couldn't hang around . . . of course the others were tucked up in their air shelters. But not me. I was on the streets, braving the buzz-bombs, bobbing and weaving, trying to get a crust.' Arthur paused to reflect on his past glory. 'I suppose we were the unsung heroes of our finest hour.'

'I wish I'd been there, Arthur.'

'You'd have loved it. I was a harum-scarum nipper in the university of hard-knocks. But then I got captured.'

'The Germans?' asked Justin with awe.

'National Service,' said Arthur flatly.

'I bet you were a commando.'

'Yeah – very similar – pay corps. I always like to be where the money is.' He looked up at the building and started to chew his cigar again.

'You all right, Arthur?' asked Justin.

'Just playing a waiting game,' said Arthur as he accidentally bit off the end of his cigar.

Terry's nerves twanged as Benson rushed down the staircase. He gave a quick glance to the right and left – and then passed a package to Terry, who tucked it into his jacket. Then they both began to walk briskly to the exit.

A few minutes later an excitable Arthur was ripping the package apart in the back of the Jag, while Terry drove. Then, as if holding up some religious artefact, he picked up the first ticket, fondled it, examined it and held it up to the light.

'Gold dust,' he said, almost salivating. Then his paranoia returned. 'Anybody following us?'

'No. Why should they?' asked Terry.

'When them little Jocks see this lot – they'll drool,' he chuckled.

'You're drooling a bit yourself,' pointed out Terry.

'Why not, eh? Now we're off to bonny Scotland.' He turned to Justin. 'Get me the briefcase, son.'

Justin picked up the executive briefcase from the back seat and humbly handed it to Arthur.

'I don't want to go to Scotland,' said Benson unhappily.

'Then you don't get weighed-in,' replied Arthur mercilessly, putting the tickets in the briefcase and locking it.

'Why?'

'I need help. I mean –' He gazed at Benson in annoyance at his lack of understanding. 'D'you think I'm going to the mean streets of Glasgie on me tod? They don't take prisoners up there, you know. What chances have I got with two thousand tickets?' But Benson was still looking uncooperative. 'I'll tell you what, I'll end up wearing a Blue Circle overcoat and having a quick paddle in the Clyde.' He gave Benson an admonishing look. 'For a few days, Benson, it's down to man-to-man marking.'

Neurotically, Arthur then tried to open the case just to check the tickets were still there. He twiddled the locks – but in vain.

'Oh my gawd,' he said, 'I can't remember the combination.'

Terry was instructed by Arthur to hire a minibus for the great trip North, so that he could be flanked by all his troops. Arthur drove, with passengers Terry, Alisdair and Benson, as they had yet to pick up Justin from the tender clutches of his glamorous mother.

'They all use them in Scotland. Very handy vehicle, you know – when they're shooting,' Arthur explained to his passengers.

Alisdair, looking up from his *Financial Times*, said, 'What d'you mean? We don't shoot in Glasgow.'

'I mean in the *country*. Up in the lochs and the braes and the Alps. With the lairds on their estates when they shoot pheasant and grouse and smoked salmon.'

Alisdair looked at Arthur's back grimly and Terry wondered how long he would contain himself.

When they drew up outside Justin's flat, Arthur said to Terry, 'Give him a shout.'

Terry got out of the minibus and approached Justin's flat. He knocked on the door and it was answered by Mrs James.

'Is he in?'

'He'll be back in a minute,' she said. 'You'd better wait.'

Reluctantly, Terry went inside, followed by Mrs James, who was wearing a dressing gown. After a quick glance in the mirror, she patted her hair and said, 'He's off to Scotland now, is he?'

'Couple of days.'

She lit a cigarette. 'I usually work – but if he's out of the house I try to relax. It's so quiet.'

'Oh yeah?' said Terry cautiously.

'More trouble, I suppose?'

'I wouldn't think so,' he said trying to reassure her – and failing.

'It's trouble,' said Mrs James. 'I can smell it.'

'You worried about him?'

'He's so restless. I mean why can't he be unemployed like everybody else? He's on remand, you know.'

'Six months, he reckons.'

'I'd be delighted if he went away for two years.'

Terry looked at Justin's mum in surprise. 'You don't want that, do you?'

'Don't I?' she said cynically. 'If he's palled up with Arthur Daley he'll probably be away for ten years.'

'You know Arthur?'

'Years ago. Right Jack the lad – bit like my Justin. Mind you I was just a kid then. I worked at the Cabaret Club in Jermyn Street. I didn't have a lot of luck – I was the hat check girl and suddenly people stopped wearing hats –'

'Arthur still wears a hat,' said Terry innocently.

'He would. Then I was a cigarette girl – and all of a sudden people stopped smoking. That's when I decided to have Justin.'

'That was nice.'

'I couldn't think of anything else to do. Want a drink?'

'Bit early for me.'

Notwithstanding, Mrs James opened a sideboard and took out the sherry bottle. The front door opened and she hurriedly put back the bottle as Justin appeared, carrying an overnight bag.

'Sorry, Tel. I suddenly realised I didn't have a bag. Nice, innit? Came from Gucci.' He glanced at his mother and then returned his gaze to Terry. 'Didn't she give you a cup of tea?'

'We've got to shoot,' said Terry hurriedly.

'Be right with you,' said Justin, dashing into his room.

'Busy boy, isn't he?' commented Mrs James. 'He was good at scripture in school, though.'

'Oh, that's handy,' said Terry, stuck for a reply.

'There's only one Archbishop isn't there?'
Terry nodded.
'I could have been croupier but for him. I mean Justin, not the Archbishop. Everybody was swinging down the Kings Road and there I was dusting talcum on his bum. I took a wrong turn somewhere.'
To Terry's relief, Justin appeared in the doorway. '*Avanti* . . . OK?'
'Nice to meet you, Mrs James –' Hurriedly Terry went to the door, while Justin said to his mother:
'You haven't been talking to my friends, have you?'
'Just "hallo",' she said casually.
'I've told you – don't talk to my friends, right?' He was about to follow Terry through the door, but he hesitated: 'You haven't got a tenner, have you?'
Defeated, Mrs James pointed to her handbag.

Arthur's minibus, driven by Terry, sped past a sign pointing to the North. Traffic was busy and so far they had all failed to notice that they were being followed by Little Phil's Cadillac.
'Got your passport, Terry? And your phrase book?' asked Arthur, who seemed to be in rare good humour.
'What you on about?'
'All foreigners from now on. Nobody speaks English north of Tottenham. Didn't your mum ever tell you that?'
'Pack it in, Arthur, I'm trying to drive.'
'Oh, is that what you call it?'
A few hours later Arthur's directions came to grief when the minibus left the motorway at Birmingham's spaghetti junction.
'You're barmy, Arthur,' said Terry.
'I'm telling you we should've stayed on the M1. Everyone knows the M1 goes to Scotland.'
'Yeah, but not Glasgow.'
'That's in Scotland, innit?'
'I give up. You'll drive me potty.'
Alisdair interrupted with an edge to his clipped voice. 'M6

for Glasgow – Terry's right, Arthur.'

Arthur shrugged, 'If you'd only consulted me earlier.'

'We did,' said Alisdair menacingly.

Back on the right motorway, Arthur took over the driving amidst an oppressive silence. But he did not allow this to affect his sunny mood. 'Cows,' he said, looking out at the open countryside.

'Do what?' asked Terry sleepily. Alisdair did not deign to reply and Justin merely looked bemused, while Benson slept.

'Cows.'

'Oh . . . great.'

'Don't knock cows.'

'It's just that they're not the most riveting topic of conversation.'

'I don't know so much – there's milk, cream, cheese and . . . er . . .'

'Yoghurt,' added Terry.

'There you are, then.'

'Yeah and that's it. End of conversation.'

There was a long pause while Arthur stared ahead. In the end he said, 'You're right.'

'Any chance of driving slower?' asked Justin. He looked ill.

'I'm only doing seventy . . . that's all.' Arthur seemed indignant.

' 'Cause I feel a bit sick.'

'Gawd. Open the window.'

Alisdair shifted away from Justin. 'Don't you dare spew over my *Financial Times*.'

'It's just a bit close in here.'

'Don't think about it, Justin,' said Arthur. 'It's all in the mind. Just concentrate –'

Justin burped. 'What on?'

'Why don't you collect numbers? You and Terry could have a competition – who can get the most Maestros?' He sounded happy in his generosity.

'Have you got any Smarties – for the winner?' asked Terry.

'You can have a touch of haggis when we get there,' Arthur promised.

Meanwhile, a few miles behind them, Cedric drove Little Phil in his Cadillac with both speed and restraint. Soon, they were crossing the Scottish border, still keeping their distance from Arthur's minibus. It was a good thing they did, for the minibus was beginning to cough and wheeze and Arthur began to nurse the clattering vehicle along, much to the disgust of its passengers.

'Overheating,' said Arthur.

'Amongst other things,' replied Terry.

The others maintained a pessimistic silence.

'There's a service area coming,' said Arthur. 'I might drop in.'

'I should,' said Alisdair, 'before the whole thing conks out.'

'Up your kilt,' muttered Arthur.

'What was that?' The edge had returned to Alisdair's voice and this time rather more sharply.

'I said – jolly good idea,' said Arthur. 'I'll soon get us back on the road.'

'On foot?' asked Terry unhelpfully.

Ten minutes later, the bonnet of the minibus was up and Arthur was in deep conversation with a middle-aged mechanic, a roll-up stuck to his lower lip.

'Can you have a look at this, squire?'

'Gasket,' said the mechanic without even looking under the bonnet.

'You haven't had a look at it yet,' said Arthur plaintively.

'Gasket – and the thermostat,' he added.

'I'm in the trade, squire,' Arthur stated knowingly. 'How long?'

'Couple of hours.'

'I'm going to Scotland.'

'Are you in the AA?'

'I told you – I'm trade, squire.'

But the mechanic was not impressed. 'It's still got to be two hours. I've got to get the spares. There isn't another garage for twenty-two miles.'

'I'll tell you what, squire . . . there's a good drink in it.'

'Thanks . . . it'll be about one hour and fifty minutes.'

Arthur gave him a searching look.

Meanwhile, Benson, Justin and Alisdair were about to enter the restaurant. Terry, anxious for news, came over to Arthur, overhearing the last part of the conversation.

'What's all this *squire* business?'

'We're in the North. The rustics love the touch.'

They walked together to the entrance of the restaurant. Then Arthur froze. 'Where's the tickets?'

'I thought you had –'

In a flash Arthur was gone, running back to the minibus. Terry followed him casually. Frantically, Arthur wrenched open the driver's door. He scrabbled in the back and retrieved his precious briefcase. When he returned to Terry, Arthur looked almost ashen.

'Don't you ever do that again.'

'Me?'

'You've gotta take care of your old Arthur.'

'Oh my Gawd.' Terry looked as if he was literally squirming.

'We're in Scotland now, the bad lands, with Apaches lurking around every corner.' Arthur glanced about him. 'Look at it – it's a wilderness. No wonder that Adrian didn't fancy it and he didn't have any football tickets.'

'You're a bit edgy, Arthur.'

'No wonder. We should've had an armoured car.' He patted the briefcase and looked around him again. 'We're talking about fifty grand at street value. Never mind about illegal substances – them wee Jocks would kill for these. And that Alisdair . . . Always reading his *Financial Times* – what's he up to? You should keep your eye on him.'

'Yes, major.'

Arthur began to march back towards the restaurant. Then, once again, he froze.

'Now what's up?' asked Terry.

Arthur pointed a shuddering finger. 'Look!' he gasped as Little Phil's Cadillac drove into the service area and parked. Arthur looked wildly at Terry. 'Did you see his little eyes? Now you wonder why I'm worried? This has got to be the furthest north he's been beyond Hendon Way. *He's* after *me*.'

And Arthur began to run for cover.

The five gallant travellers had gathered together in a corner of the garish motorway cafe. Dominated by their plastic world, they were subdued. Under the yellow neon, they ate without pleasure and talked dispassionately.

'What I really fancied was a Pina Colada,' said Justin. No-one replied.

Alisdair wiped his mouth. 'I think I'll call Glasgow,' he said, going to the door.

'Follow him,' whispered Arthur to Terry.

'Why?'

'To see what he's doing?'

'He's going to phone somebody. What's the big deal?'

'I just want to know,' said Arthur between gritted teeth, his eyes alive with paranoia and suspicion.

But Terry clearly wasn't going to move. Arthur grabbed the briefcase and walked to the door. Outside the entrance to the toilets, there were two public pay phones. Alisdair was talking into one of them. Hurriedly, Arthur returned to the corner table and whispered urgently to Terry:

'He's talking to somebody on the dog and bone.'

Terry looked at him. 'So that's how he does it.'

'Eh?'

'I thought he was going to shout. But he uses the phone instead.'

Arthur sat down heavily. 'I wonder who he's talking to?'

'How do I know?' said Terry irritably.

Arthur scowled at him, picked up his plastic cup and grimaced as he drank. At that moment Cedric came in. He saw them and gave Arthur a patronising smile. He then went to the counter and bought two teas.

Justin glanced at Arthur. 'D'you know him?'

Arthur nodded.

'And what about you?' asked Terry.

'Well I . . . I had to tell him –' Justin said uncomfortably.

'What?' Arthur's voice was hollow.

'About us – and the tickets.'

'Thank you!'

'He was going to give me a hammering. So I told him –'

'What did you tell him?' asked Arthur in a distant voice.

'You have to settle with *him* – I said. The guv'nor, the don of all dons. He wasn't all that impressed.'

'You didn't say it in Italian, did you?'

'I haven't got to that bit in the phrase book. Anyway, you're not worried, are you? What about the old days when you was in gang warfare at Brighton racecourse?'

'That was before the war.'

'Was it? Well, what about the street corner bookmakers – the shoot-out at Mister Smith's – you know, the what-d'ye-call-it family, and the what's-'is-name twins –'

Arthur studied Justin for a moment with confirmed distaste. 'Justin, your yearning for nostalgia is almost morbid.'

'I'm just trying to learn, aren't I?'

'The first lesson is to say nothing to nobody.' He leant back in his chair and closed his eyes as if trying to blot out the harsh realities of the material world.

'He was gonna strangle me,' said Justin excitedly.

'Particularly to people who are going to strangle you,' said Arthur in a sonorous voice. Then instinct made him open his eyes and he was back to reality.

Cedric was approaching him, carrying plastic cups and two fruit buns. He stopped three or four yards away from their table. 'Phil would like to see you,' he said.

'I'm here,' said Arthur with a detachment he didn't feel. He gave a quick glance to Justin just to ensure that he knew he was in command of the situation.

'We tried to find you last night,' said Cedric. 'Went to the usual haunts, but you had an early night. Imagine you on the high road to Scotland –' He ended on a note of wonderment.

'It's the Winchester Annual Trip,' said Arthur.

'Well – Phil's in his Cadillac, looking at the afternoon film.'

'What's that? *Stranger in the Night*?' asked Terry innocently.

'Mister Daley is in a meeting,' said Justin.

Cedric leant forward threateningly. 'I'll shove this fruit bun down your throat if you don't watch it, sonny.'

Justin turned to appeal to everybody. 'See what I mean?' His voice rose hysterically.

'Justin – reduce the volume,' said Arthur censoriously. He looked up at Cedric. 'I'll be there directly.'

Cedric stared at Justin for a second and then went away. Before he was out of earshot, Justin said:

'Yeah – and *buona notte*.'

Cedric hesitated, scowled and then walked on.

'That's "goodnight",' said Terry.

'Is it . . .? Well, he didn't know that, did he?'

Arthur lit a cigar and then rose majestically to his feet, nodding at Terry as he did so. Reluctantly, Terry also rose. Arthur was ready to meet Little Phil.

As they walked towards the door their progress was interrupted by a dishevelled young Scots fan, wearing a tam-o'-shanter and tartan scarf.

'Hey Jimmy . . . gie's a light?'

Arthur offered the glowing tip of his cigar and the fan lit his cigarette.

'Nice game, was it?' asked Arthur casually, trying to ensure that the still observant Justin did not think he was in too much of a hurry to obey Little Phil's summons.

'What game?' asked the fan.

'I assume you've been at a football match?'

'That was two years ago . . . Hamburg. D'you think they've kept my job open?'

'No, but you'll get a nice Giro cheque.'

Arthur continued his stately progress to the door, followed by a yawning Terry.

As Terry and Arthur walked towards the car park, Arthur

said, 'He'd have bought a ticket.'

'Yeah – but what about Little Phil?'

Arthur gave the briefcase to Terry. 'Guard this with your life.' He straightened his jacket. 'And don't worry about me. I'm bigger than Little Phil.' Arthur touched Terry's arm and gave a brave smile. 'I'll be okay now – just cover me.'

'I will,' said Terry dramatically. 'Just get out of the burning sun, Arthur – and watch his right arm.'

Frowning at Terry's frivolity, Arthur walked alone towards Phil's Cadillac.

As Terry walked back to the restaurant, a group, of young people passed him. Amongst them, he saw a girl smile.

'Sorry – do I know you?'

'Inland Revenue.'

Terry started back. It was Miss Demosthenous from the Inland Revenue. Instantly, he looked at her legs, only to discover she was wearing jeans.

'How are you?' asked Terry, but too late, for she had hurried on.

Justin was washing his hands in the toilets when Alisdair burst into the room. His first action was to grab Justin and fling him against the wash basins.

'You're a lucky man.'

Justin sprawled on the floor, staring up at him in terror. 'You gone potty?'

'I've got egg on my face and you're going to have blood on your throat –'

'Leave it out. What have I done?' On his hands and knees Justin tried to crawl to the door. As he did so, he received a sharp, painful kick on the backside from Alisdair.

'You must think we're mental up here, don't you?'

At that moment the doors opened and a traveller entered. He was suitably surprised by what he saw.

Alisdair gave him a sweet smile and said, 'We're just friends, you know.'

'Well, in that case, I'll come back later.' The traveller

closed the door firmly behind him and from his position on the floor, Justin said:

'You've got the hump, haven't you?'

'I'm a civilised man, an accountant. I don't do things like this. I don't kick people around toilets.'

'Then why don't you stop?' Justin asked.

'I went to an Academy – I've got letters after my name.'

'Which ones?'

Alisdair aimed a wild kick at him, which Justin just avoided.

'Forgeries! How could you do it?' Alisdair's voice was calmer.

'Them tickets?' Justin stared at him in surprise.

'I've been on the phone since we came here – they know, they know.' He ended on a declamatory note.

'Who knows?'

'My people – they've got contacts, friends at Wembley. They know.'

'Blimey,' said Justin.

'They've checked the postal applications and there are no missing tickets. You're flogging forgeries.'

Justin sagged against the wall. 'I don't believe it.'

Alisdair looked at him with the bitterness of a disappointed father. 'You're just a *boy*. Oh aye . . . you've mixed with the wrong people all right – Arthur Daley, Terry McCann –'

'They don't know about it, either. Benno – he got them into this.'

Alisdair gave a resigned scowl. 'I remember him when he was playing – always diving in the penalty box.'

'Well – he can't claim "foul" this time.' Justin tried to get on his feet, backing off as Alisdair came towards him. But this time he was trying to help him.

As Alisdair pulled Justin to his feet, he said, 'Sorry about the violence.'

'Well,' said Justin, 'it wasn't very nice.'

Alisdair gave Justin a wild look. 'We don't *do* this in Glasgow,' he said.

'Of course you don't,' said Justin respectfully.

The autograph hunter was a young man with an obsessive air and Terry knew they were in for a real dose of ear-bending when he arrived in the swirling gloom clouds of their table.

'I thought you were Steve Benson,' he said giving Benson a grubby piece of paper.

'I am,' he said, signing his name.

'I saw you against City about ten years ago. Two late goals and then you got booked. Not many like you now, eh Steve?'

'Thank you,' said Benson. The young man smiled gratefully and went away, whilst Benson grinned up at Terry, his mood lightening a little.

'He's got a good memory . . . eh?'

'Ever thought of getting into management?'

'What, with my record? They want stable characters – they don't want guys like me – been in the gossip columns, in court, into scrapes – I'd be a bad influence. And if you're going to say "Why don't you get a pub?" – I've had a couple, plus a restaurant and a sports shop.'

'America?'

'They don't want to know. Got any other ideas?'

'Mini-cabbing?'

'Lost me licence two years ago –'

Benson saw Justin and Alisdair approaching. 'We're talking about my career, Justin. They shoot horses, don't they?' he said cheerily.

But Justin was in no mood for jocularity. 'Shooting's too good for you,' he said.

'What?' Benson was astonished.

'You're just a professional toe-rag, ain't you?' remarked Justin sweetly.

Meanwhile, inside the large Cadillac in the Service Area's car-park, Little Phil and Arthur were watching a portable TV set.

'I like George Formby as well,' said Arthur.

'And Will Hay. I mean, it's better than racing,' said Little Phil nostalgically. Then his mood changed. 'Have I done anything against you?' he asked.

'Never, Phil,' replied Arthur resolutely.

'I got an electronic carving knife from you couple of years back. No complaints.'

'That was a snip. I'd like to get some more if I could.'

'Course you would,' said Little Phil generously. 'To each his own. For your own reasons you've diversified into electronic carving knives, motors, antiques, hi-fi, whatever. And now tickets as well. Myself, I concentrate on one market – a business I know – tickets.'

'You're an expert, Phil. The best scalper in the game,' said Arthur with all the respect of one pro for another.

Little Phil replied patiently, 'I don't like that word scalper, or even tout. I think of myself as a ticket *broker*. You want to go to *The Mousetrap*, not my taste, but I can fix you up. Russian ballet, which I *do* like, or two together for old blue eyes' umpteenth farewell concert – no problem. Give me a bell and I'm happy to comply.'

'You're well known for it,' remarked Arthur with the same professional respect.

'Precisely. I've got four hundred tickets for the England-Scotland game, but that's not enough. Then I meet you on the motorway by chance and you say you've got two *thousand*. You see, Arthur, it's all a question of *respect*. I'm known as the man who runs the ticket market – that's why I'm going to Glasgow. Suddenly, Arthur, you're a threat.'

'Me?'

'And a threat has to be curtailed – or destroyed.'

Arthur considered his statement for a few seconds. Then he said, 'As you explain it, I can understand your problem.'

'Not my problem – your problem. It's peace or war, you know that, Arthur.'

Arthur spoke in a measured, reflective tone. 'To be honest, Phil, I'm not all that crazy about the ticket business. I don't trust them little Jocks anyway.'

'You have to understand minorities, Arthur.'

'And you've got the gift. You can have 'em.'

'I can?'

'Yeah, you can have the two thousand eight pound seats for thirty-five grand.'

Little Phil smiled as if he had just heard a very good joke. A little old perhaps, but very good. 'You're talking silly money, Arthur. I'll give you half.'

'I need a small margin of profit,' Arthur protested.

'Twenty.'

'Twenty-five?'

'Arthur – we're business men –'

At that moment, Cedric rapped on the car window. 'It's Benno,' he mouthed.

Looking out of their cosy eyrie, Little Phil and Arthur watched Benson pass them, running like an Olympic sprinter. A few paces behind him was Terry.

'Taking exercise, are they?' asked Little Phil.

'He ain't jogging,' replied Arthur.

Benson was running down a slip road now with Terry hard on his heels. Avoiding a stream of traffic, he jumped over a fence and ran on into a woodland, with Terry closing on him.

'You can't run all the way to London,' Terry shouted.

But Benson showed no sign of hearing and the race became something of a steeplechase as they both tore through the wood, leaping over felled branches and tangled briars. Gradually, Terry narrowed the gap until Benson, aware that his stamina was at an end, turned to kick Terry and grab at his jacket.

'You'll get booked for that,' panted Terry as he brought him down. They both sprawled on the ground – in the middle of a large puddle.

As he lay in the water, feeling it seep into his clothes, Terry said, 'I hope you haven't spent all that money.'

Meanwhile, in the Cadillac, the atmosphere had changed perceptively. Little Phil seemed to have been very shaken by the enthusiastic athletics he had just witnessed.

'What about our deal then, Phil?' asked Arthur hopefully, knowing full well that all could be lost.

'Oh, I don't know.' His eyes returned to the flickering screen. 'There might be a stewards' inquiry now.'

Arthur closed his eyes. It was true – reality was too disappointing. He needed a holiday.

Arthur drove the minibus in the slow lane back down the motorway with Terry beside him. Justin and Benson were in the back. Alisdair, with tight lips, had hitched a lift north.

Finally, Arthur broke the silence by saying, 'How could you do a thing like that, eh?'

'I don't know,' said Benson.

'A professional foul?' asked Terry.

'Something like that. You get desperate, don't you?'

'What about that bloke at Wembley?' asked Arthur. 'Your contact?'

'There wasn't a contact. I stashed the tickets in the loo the night before,' replied Benson disconsolately.

'It gets worse.'

'We nearly got away with it.'

'*We?*' asked Arthur. 'What do you mean, *we?*'

'You would've taken the dough.'

'I almost had a deal with Little Phil.' Arthur sounded reflective.

'But that would have been dishonest, wouldn't it?' put in Terry.

'I didn't know that they were forgeries – not at that point.'

'Anyway, you'll get your money back,' said Benson consolingly.

But Arthur was not to be appeased. 'And what about the three per cent interest on the eighteen grand? The petrol and the new gasket, thermostat and cups of tea and pies and biscuits and all the aggravation?'

'That's right,' said Justin. 'In the old days it would've been a kneecap job, wouldn't it, Arthur?'

Arthur scowled at him in the driving mirror.

Justin continued unabashed. 'I'll tell you what, Arthur. I'll make it up to you when I come out. I mean, we're going to be partners anyway, so –'

'Justin.'

'Yes, Arthur?'

'I don't want to see, or hear from you ever again.'

'You must be kidding? Just as we were getting on so well.'

'As they say, Justin. This is *finito*.'

Justin sat there, unable to believe what Arthur was saying.

Terry tried to translate. 'I think he means *ciao* – and all that.'

PART TWO

Dreams of big money had always haunted Arthur, but after the Wembley tickets fiasco he went to ground for a while, nursing his disappointment and cursing Justin.

Terry, meanwhile, with little to do for Arthur, was forced to resort to the part-time work he had so vividly described to the income tax inspector.

'Can't you find nothing to do?' asked Big John officiously as he bustled past Terry.

'All seems very quiet – apart from the music.' Terry looked around the night-spot with its young band, centre stage, and its gyrating dancers on the floor. It was an all too familiar scene, for he knew there was no money in bouncing. It was something he was forced back on every time Arthur licked his wounds.

Big John paused, sensing a challenge in Terry's casual attitude. Asserting himself, he said, 'Well keep an eye on that little team at the bar. They look like trouble-makers to me.'

Terry glanced in the direction of the bar, seeing a group of youths laughing and drinking. They looked harmless enough, but to keep the peace, he said, 'Anything you say, chief.'

Big John went on his way, whilst Terry glanced at the bar again. But there was no problem.

The final thundering chords came from the band, the sweating musicians took their bow and the crowd cheered. Then they trooped off stage with their instruments.

Backstage, Chris Lambert picked his way carefully among the instruments and amplifiers. He was one of a new breed of impressarios – young, brash and confident. As he arrived the young members of the group were mopping themselves down, swigging coke and packing up their gear. Chris walked up to their leader.

'Good gig, Barry. You'll definitely get an invite back.'

'Great.'

He handed Barry four fivers.

'Twenty?' he asked in surprise.

'Something the matter?'

'We were told we were getting seventy.'

'Who told you that?'

Barry turned to his drummer. 'You said seventy, didn't you, Sammy?'

'That's what you said, Chris, when I fixed the gig.'

Chris's reaction was one of both astonishment and amusement. 'Seventy? I said seventy? Hey, John, they think they're superstars.' He turned round as Big John loomed out of the shadows. Then he continued, looking reassured. 'Be sensible. How can I pay a bunch of kids like you seventy?'

'Twenty's hardly worth our while,' said Barry unhappily. 'Knock off the transport and we're left with about two quid each.'

Chris shook his head sadly. 'I don't understand you kids,' he said paternally. 'You spend most of your time on the social security and I give you a chance by putting you on in a big establishment. I give you exposure to a large public, an opportunity to build up a personal following. What else can I do? You do want an invite back, don't you?'

'Naturally,' said Barry defensively.

'Then take your twenty.'

Barry took the money and stuffed it into his shirt pocket.

'And show a bit of gratitude as well,' said Big John softly.

'We don't want any aggravation, John. It's been a genuine misunderstanding – right, Barry?' said Chris.

Barry gave him a resigned look. 'Sure,' he said.

Chris smiled engagingly. 'I think you went down quite well. Really nice.'

'Thanks.'

'So listen. Drop in in a couple of days and we'll talk about another gig. OK?'

'Yeah, OK.' He paused. 'Thanks a lot, Chris.'

'It's OK. See you fellers.' Chris gave a cheery wave, then he departed with Big John at his side.

Once they had gone, Barry turned to his band. 'What a stitch-up,' he said.

It was the end of a sweaty evening. The record faded out, the lights went up and the disco suddenly became its barren and tawdry self. Almost instantly the bars were shuttered, glasses were gathered in and ashtrays emptied. On the PA a voice, originally welcoming and full of bonhomie, snarled. 'OK, we're closing the club now. That's all for tonight.'

Most customers took the hint and began to depart, but one remained disgruntled: for young Alan had suddenly realised that not only was the disco finished, but his glass had gone and with it, a double Bacardi and Coke.

'It doesn't matter, Alan,' said his girl-friend when Alan began to protest.

'Doesn't matter? You're kidding, I've just lost a full Bacardi and Coke.' He turned to the massive bulk of Big John who was chivvying the punters out as quickly as he could. 'Excuse me. I had a full drink there. They seem to have taken it away.' He was polite, but forceful.

'Well, we're closed, ain't we? We're not an all-night bloody drinking club.'

'But I hadn't even touched that drink.'

Big John jabbed a finger into the boy's ribs. 'Shut up and get out.'

'Listen,' he said reasonably, 'I had –'

But this seemed enough provocation for Big John to grab him by the shirt front. 'You trying to make trouble?'

'I'm going to complain about you,' said Alan indignantly. 'Take your hands off me.' He tried to push Big John away – a fatal move for Big John immediately slammed him against the wall.

'Cheeky sod,' said Big John. Then, as Alan rebounded from the wall, he punched him in the face and blood burst from the boy's nose. The girl-friend screamed as Big John piled into Alan again. Two of their friends watched in horror, but made no move to interfere as Alan's girl-friend continued to scream her head off.

'Come on the lot of you . . . out of it,' said Big John as he half dragged, half carried Alan to a side exit, while his girl-friend yelled:

'I'm going to report you to the police.'

'Shut up, you little slag, and get out.' He favoured her with a particularly brutal grin as he shoved her through the exit and slammed the door. Glaring round at any other customers who might be loitering, he saw Terry, who, drawn by the commotion, had arrived on the scene and was cynically watching Big John.

'You was a big help.'

'Well, they didn't exactly seem like the Wild Bunch, did they?' he said drily. 'Now who do I see about getting paid out?'

'Me.'

'Well?'

Big John pulled a wad of notes from his pocket, peeled off two fivers and handed them to Terry.

'It's three of them innit?'

'Tenner.'

Terry came a little closer to Big John who, despite his size, looked wary. 'Plus five for the VAT,' he said.

'Now look, pal –'

Terry came a little closer. 'Never mind "look". Mate of mine asked me to stand in for him. Three fivers – that's what he said and that's what I walk out of here with. OK?'

There was something about Terry's quiet confidence that worried Big John. Grumbling, he extracted a grimy looking fiver. 'And tell your pal, if he can't make it any more, *I'll* find a deputy.'

'With the money you're paying you'll probably get Muhammad Ali. Tara, chief,' said Terry as he headed for the door.

Big John watched him go, mentally marking him down.

Terry sat beside Arthur as he drove his Jag slowly through the crowded streets. He seemed to have recovered something of his optimism – always a sign to Terry of impending trouble.

'You will get yourself involved in these dopey jobs.'

Terry had just been giving Arthur a dour account of last night's action at the disco.

'Dennis wanted a night off.'

'He's going to have two years off,' said Arthur complacently.

'Eh?'

'Didn't you see the papers? There were four of 'em. They thought they'd had it away with a Belgian juggernaut and there were six Old Bill sitting in the back.' Arthur paused. 'Your name was up for that an' all.'

'That's nice.'

'I told 'em. Not my Terry. He don't want to know about pickaxe handles and shooters – not him.'

Arthur turned the Jag into a mews that had arches running below a railway line. Most of them were filled with workshops and small warehouses – all of which were grubby and run-down.

Arthur slowed the Jag down and said, ' "Not that we've joined the other side," I said. "All we've done is like Sweden in the war – we've declared our neutrality." ' Then he braked sharply. 'Blimey.'

Parked across the mews was a police Rover 3500 with a uniformed constable standing by the car. Examining the doors to a lock-up storeroom was a plain-clothed detective who looked all too familiar.

Terry turned to Arthur. 'What have you been up to, Arthur?'

'Shtum, Terry. Very, very shtum.'

Arthur got slowly out of the car and approached his old friend, Detective Sergeant Chisholm, who smiled up at Arthur in the friendliest manner. 'I never knew this was your gaff, Arthur?'

'I never said it was. Something the matter, Mister Chisholm?'

'We've got no record of you as landlord, tenant or registered key holder,' he said, ignoring Arthur's badly concealed irritation.

'What's the problem?'

'You've had the burglars round – that's the problem.' He chuckled slightly.

Arthur stared at the door. It was double padlocked, but the hasp for one of the padlocks had been severed.

'Catch 'em?'

Chisholm grinned and shook his head. 'Patrol car spotted 'em. But we're not sure . . . were they coming out, or still trying to get in? It *is* your place, is it?'

'Sort of,' said Arthur cagily.

'Well, let's have a look inside and we'll see if they got away with anything –'

'I don't think that's necessary,' said Arthur very quickly as Chisholm gave him a knowing look.

'What've you got in there, Arthur?'

He shrugged as if to diminish Chisholm's interest. But he only served to increase it. 'Odds and ends. Very nice of you fellers taking an interest. I'll let you know if there's anything missing.'

Arthur made no move to open the padlock and Chisholm waited patiently, but determinedly. 'We'll just have a peek, Arthur.'

'I'll take an inventory,' said Arthur. 'Don't bother yourself, Mr Chisholm.'

Finally, and regretfully, Chisholm realised he was getting nowhere with Arthur – for the moment, at least.

'I wonder what they'd be after, Arthur?' he asked ruminatively.

'Gawd knows, Mister Chisholm. Probably just kids. You know what the younger generation is like nowadays.'

'I still think we should have a look though.' He was trying again for the last time.

Arthur gave him a reassuring grin. 'Normally, I wouldn't mind, Mister Chisholm. But the place is such a mess.'

There was a long pause, at the end of which, Chisholm said dryly, 'All right, Arthur.' He turned away regretfully, walked to the car and then glanced back at Arthur. 'You'll be well insured, I suppose?'

'No worries.'

'The Royal?'

'No.' He pointed to Terry. 'Himself.'

Terry was leaning against Arthur's car and he gave Chisholm a pleasant nod.

'Just remember, Arthur, if you're going away for the weekend, don't forget to inform your local police station,' said Chisholm.

Terry smiled and muttered to him, 'Then you're a certainty to get your gaff turned over. See you, Mister Chisholm.' Terry joined Arthur as they watched Detective Sergeant Chisholm get into the car. As he did so, a man in overalls in the workshop next door, quickly slipped a pile of car number plates under some rubbish. The visit had been unwelcome all round.

Arthur watched the police car leave the mews. He took a key ring from his pocket and inserted it into the undamaged padlock. 'No wonder Sir Keith Joseph's always on about law 'n' order, Terry. Everywhere you go there's tea-leafs.' He opened the door and stepped into the darkness.

Arthur switched on the light, illuminating an Aladdin's cave of treasures, all of which he regarded as highly saleable commodities. One wall was stacked high with unopened cases of Smirnoff vodka, another with TV sets, transistor radios, washing machines. There were three clothes rails with Oscar Jacobson suits and neatly packaged shirts were in piles on the floor. A stack of books in one corner and a display rack of ties completed the range.

Arthur beamed at Terry, anticipating compliments. But he did not receive any. 'You're at the long firm again,' said Terry.

'What're you talking about? I paid for all this lot.' He looked very offended.

'Bent gear. You're going to get us nicked again.'

'Terry, this is all strictly kosher.'

'Then why didn't you want the law to have a look?'

For a moment, just a brief moment, Arthur looked a trifle

uncomfortable. 'Cos it's nothing to do with them, that's why. Do you think they have the law nosing around every five minutes at Harrods?'

Terry sighed deeply, not believing Arthur for one moment. Morosely, he glanced round at the merchandise.

'Nice suits,' said Arthur encouragingly. 'Swedish. You like a nice Oscar Jacobson, don't you?' He selected a suit from the rail, slipped the jacket from the hanger and offered it to Terry. 'That's about your size.'

Despite himself, Terry tried on the jacket.

'Nice. Hundred and thirty in the shops. You look the business in that, son. No problem.'

'Good cut,' Terry said grudgingly.

'Yeah – you can have that one for seventy.'

'How much?' asked Terry looking shocked.

'All right. Give us fifty then,' compromised Arthur.

'Bent gear –'

'Terry, on my landlord's life. The whole lot is straight,' said Arthur vehemently. 'I got bills of sale, receipts – everything.'

'Where?'

'The feller's bringing them round. All I done was buy a job lot and the container burst –' Arthur's explanation was a trifle rapid.

Terry was silent and Arthur said, 'Obviously, it's all export stuff.'

'Export!' He examined the jacket. 'These are *from* Sweden.'

'Exports and imports. That's what I mean. What about these then?' With a sense of triumph he flourished a book from the stack in the corner. 'Five hundred digest versions of *Great Expectations* by Charles bleeding Dickens. You can't say *they're* Swedish, can you?'

Terry gazed at him thoughtfully and then gave up, giving Arthur the opportunity to briskly start the next move.

'Now, what we got to do is to think about shifting it all and getting some better locks for that door.' He sat down on a pile of shirts. 'And then,' he said, 'we've got to work out who sussed the gear was here and tried to get in.'

Terry was trying on another jacket. 'Course it wouldn't be

a few pals of the bloke you bought it from?' asked Terry innocently.

'It might be,' said Arthur with sudden, surprising honesty. 'That's why we've got to start clearing it, fast.'

An hour later, Arthur's Jag pulled up outside a large pub. Arthur then lifted out two cases of Smirnoff and stacked them in Terry's arms. 'I'm knocking these out for two pounds a bottle. That's about right, isn't it?'

'You go in tonight and have three doubles and you'll 've bought one back. How about that?' He went over to the pub, pushed the door with his foot and went inside.

Meanwhile, the true impact of Terry's remark dawned on Arthur. 'Bloody publicans. Three weeks and I'll be out of pocket.'

Inside the large music lounge just off the main bar of the pub, Freddie, the landlord, was sitting at a table listening to a girl singer accompanied by a pianist. He was looking pained, for although the girl was young and attractive, her singing was atrocious. The pianist was labouring not only to keep in time with her but also to keep in the same key. Sitting beside Freddie was the girl's boy-friend and agent, a little hustler in his mid-twenties. He was whispering:

'She's into nostalgia . . . see.'

'Yeah,' said Freddie.

Meanwhile, Terry was stacking the Smirnoff boxes by the bar, almost unable to believe how badly she was murdering the 'sixties ballad. Then Arthur appeared behind him, carrying the last of the boxes.

'Good way to close a pub, innit?' said Terry.

But there was no immediate response from Arthur and when Terry glanced at him, he saw Arthur was transfixed.

'Now that's what I call a song, Terry.'

'Eh?'

'And a knock-out bird an' all.'

'Not exactly a Capital chart-climber, is it?'

'Don't tell me you know about music for gawd's sake,' said Arthur. 'That was . . . erm . . . 1965 if I remember correctly.

Liz Taylor and what's-'is-name – the Welsh feller in the film.'

'Sixty-five?'

'Yes – the year Cassius Clay changed his name after dumping Liston in one minute of the first. I can't be faulted on my history,' he said sanctimoniously.

'Same year I dumped big Keith Perkins,' said Terry brightly.

'Who?'

'Top man at Burston Road Secondary Mod. He was good at history an' all.'

As they spoke the singer laboured to the end of the song, dragging the last word out for several beats too many. There was silence while she smiled hopefully in the direction of Freddie. Until she heard solitary clapping.

It was Arthur, beaming and unperturbed by the general lack of enthusiasm around him. 'Beautiful, knock out!' he exclaimed.

The girl have him a quick, nervous smile. 'Ta.'

Freddie shot a glance at Arthur. Then his jaundiced gaze returned to the girl. 'Well, darling, we're basically a rock and roll pub. So . . . er . . .'

'So you don't want to know . . . You're all the bloody same you lot . . .' She sounded tearful as she fled from the stage.

'Oi,' said Arthur, starting up after the girl, and laying a restraining hand on her agent's arm. 'Leave it to me, son . . .' He brushed past him and hurried after the girl into the street. 'Just a minute, luv,' he yelled.

The girl hesitated as Arthur puffed his way alongside her.

'What's your name, love?'

'Sharon – but I'm not free.'

'I thought you were.'

'Now look, sunshine –' She tried to make off again but Arthur added:

'Musically speaking, I mean.'

'Eh?' She paused again.

'Don't let that lot upset you.'

'They don't appreciate nothing good them sort.'

'Course they don't,' said Arthur reassuringly. 'But it's only a boozer, isn't it? I mean, Friday night it's full of yobboes. Your style's more some West End nighterie. Know what I mean?'

'Yeah, well that's what I think too,' she said and began to cry.

Arthur pulled out his silk handkerchief. 'Now, come on, why don't you dry them little tears. Got a motor?'

She shook her head.

'Then I'd better give you a lift home, eh, Sharon?'

Sharon spotted Arthur's Jag and was suitably impressed. With a quick smile, she nodded, dabbing at her cheeks with Arthur's hankie.

'Nice hankie.'

'Pure silk, innit? Got a couple of dozen of them indoors. Just to match all the different suits.'

Arthur gallantly walked round and opened the passenger door for Sharon. Twirling his keys, he walked round to the driver's side. Showbiz suddenly had its appeal.

Driving Sharon down the Fulham Road in his Jag, Arthur gave her a brief grin and received a coy smile in return.

'Are you in the business then?' she asked.

'I'm Arthur Daley.'

But although Arthur was hoping for instant recognition, he didn't get it.

'I'm Sharon Nightingale – not my real name of course.'

'What, Sharon?'

'No,' she giggled, 'Nightingale, but it sounds better than Dobbs anyway. But I thought you must be in the business, being so appreciative and all.'

Arthur spoke in a slow measured tone. 'I've got a lot of contacts in the – er – business, Sharon. Clubs and hotels mainly. I was having a drink with Jimmy Saville the other night at a little charity dinner we was at. Contacts is the name of the game, Sharon.'

'I know,' she said rather dolefully.

'So I could probably be a great help to you in your career.'

She nodded uncomprehendingly and Arthur, noting her

puzzled expression, tried for clarification. 'You need the right promotion,' he said. 'Proper handling –'

'That's what I think.'

'Married?'

'No.'

'Feller in the pub with you? Boy-friend?'

'Nothing like that. He wants to be an agent. He went to Pitman's Business College and everything.'

'That's nice.'

Then Sharon gasped. 'D'you see that?'

'What?' He instinctively braked.

'In that shop window. A really nice dress. Beautiful I mean.'

'Blimey. I thought you was witness to a robbery or something.'

'You couldn't stop – just so I could have a look, could you?' she asked.

'Course I could,' said Arthur gallantly, putting the car into reverse. There was some impatient horn-blowing from a car behind as the driver swerved wildly to avoid the Jag, but Arthur was quite impervious to it all. 'And you, china,' he said as the driver sped past him, giving him a generous measure of words and gestures.

Looking from the car into the window, Arthur sought the price tag and found it – a mere £120.

'It's like you said, Arthur,' said Sharon. 'Presentation is everything in this game, isn't it?'

'Course it is. Look at the gear that Shirley Bassey wears,' he said unconcernedly. 'It'd look beautiful. Why don't you try it on?'

'Oh, Arthur, should I?'

'When you're with Arthur Daley, sweetheart, it's cabaret time. Live a little . . . eh?'

But Arthur wore an expression of resignation as he helped Sharon out of the car.

Terry was underneath the arches at work on the doors of the lock-up, fixing a massive padlock on the inside. He glanced up as Arthur's Jag drove down the mews.

'Long lie-in?' asked Terry cheerily as Arthur got out.

'Some chance of that with 'er indoors 'oovering round the bed. I didn't get in till gone four.'

'Dear oh dear – not the singing scrubber?'

'What d'you call her?' He looked outraged.

'Sorry,' said Terry quickly.

'That is a very special young lady, Terence.'

'And what's her speciality?'

Arthur frowned. 'That's all you would understand – something like that. She's just a nice girl and good company at that.' He walked into the storeroom followed by Terry. There he began to examine a large pile of jeans.

'What else has she got?' persisted Terry.

'Enormous talent.'

Terry gave Arthur an old-fashioned look. 'I thought you was going to say something else for a minute.'

'You would do. I thought Jackie Strong was coming for these jeans.'

'He was and he did. But then he said those jeans with the famous label were made in Albania and'd last about two weeks. He has his reputation to think of. His reputation as an honest trader down the market – or so he says.'

'He was selling Christian Dior perfume the other week made by a little Paki in his council flat kitchen by QPR stadium, no less,' said Arthur sourly.

'You was talking about "talent",' said Terry hurriedly changing the subject.

Arthur turned on him, his eyes gleaming. 'That girl is going to be a superstar. As her manager, I'll give it two years before we'll be tax havening it in the Cayman Islands.' He sounded very confident.

'You got more chance of caravanning it down on Canvey Island,' said Terry realistically.

'You know what you know? Nothing,' said Arthur sweetly. 'What you forget is I've still got a few friends in clubland. A few favours still outstanding. So I'm going to start making a few calls.'

'Like where?'

'Top places – like the Blue Gardenia.'

'The *what?*'

'"The what?" he says.' Arthur gave Terry a deeply patronising glance. 'Only one of the most exclusive nighteries in the West End. Jermyn Street. You know where that is, don't you?'

'Arthur –'

'They have top Americans in the cabaret.'

'Arthur –'

'It's the haunt of royalty.'

'Arthur –' said Terry yet again, determined to interrupt.

'Yes,' said Arthur wearily.

'They closed that in the swinging 'sixties.'

Arthur looked dumbfounded.

'And all the other places like it.'

'The Golden Bangle –' said Arthur desperately. 'There was a lavish floorshow there.'

'Yeah, well the lavish floorshow now consists of a geezer putting on records and debs and rock stars eating hamburgers and chips.'

'All those beautiful places,' he reflected nostalgically.

'Yeah, and we lost India an' all.' Terry was not sympathetic.

'Don't wind me up on history,' said Arthur irritably.

'Sorry.'

'See, I don't do the West End much these days.'

'No,' commented Terry bleakly.

'Well, how do they make it then? All these kids . . . Top of the Pops and all that?' Arthur's voice took on a strident note.

'How would I know?'

'The place you was working in the other night. That was music, wasn't it?'

'So they said. I suppose all the groups start in pubs like that,' said Terry vaguely.

Arthur rose up in a brisk and business-like manner. 'All right. What's the guy's name? The head man?'

'How do I know? I was on the subs' bench for a bouncer.'

'You should make it a point to *know*,' said Arthur reprovingly. 'That's how you get on in the world.' He started for the door, but Terry was anxious to detain him.

'What am I supposed to be doing now?'

'Sorting out all them metric sizes into the approximate English equivalent.'

'Eh?'

Arthur paused, tapping his forehead. 'Think about it. Give them muscles up there a chance of a workout.' With a brief smile, Arthur disappeared, leaving Terry cursing behind him.

At the disco, the sound system was being tested and balanced. As a result, strange noises darted from various areas of the building and there was an occasional burst of recorded music.

Meanwhile, a couple of cleaners were at work – one pushing a jumbo size vacuum cleaner and the other wiping tables and chairs. All this activity tended to emphasise the tattiness of the sordid, evil-smelling cavern.

Big John led Arthur across the deserted auditorium. As he walked, Arthur gazed about him sceptically. There was no doubt about it – this was a far cry from Jermyn Street and nightingales singing in Berkeley Square.

As if sensing his mood, Big John said, 'When you get five hundred screaming kids in here and all the psychedelic lights are going it all looks a bit different.'

'Glad to hear it,' said Arthur addressing the bulk of Big John's rear quarters. He flinched as a particularly dreadful noise screeched from one of the mammoth loudspeakers. Then they headed towards a staircase and Arthur was ushered into Chris's office.

Autographed photographs of pop stars past and present were on the walls whilst executive toys littered the desk. Behind the vast polished surface sat Chris. His shirt was open almost to the waist and a St Christopher medallion dangled on his chest.

Arthur sat himself down in front of the desk, whilst Big

John lurked in the background.

'You probably know my name well enough. Arthur Daley.'

Chris didn't even bother to look up and began to play with one of his executive toys. 'Can't say I do really,' he said carelessly.

'Little bit out of my manor really. But I've got this fantastic girl singer.'

'Mebbe you should let me decide that –'

'What?'

'Whether she's very good. Got a demo?'

'Eh?'

'Cassette.'

'Just take my word for it.'

Chris continued to fiddle with his toy. Then he glanced up, showing Arthur the stainless steel magnetic gadget. 'They copulate, see. Like a praying mantis, only she don't turn round and eat him. Now, what exactly is the deal, Mister Daley?'

'I'd like her to go on here, so a few people can hear her. She ought to have a good band and all that.'

'Got it. Got it. You're talking about you paying us – not us paying you?'

'Mebbe I am. Depends, dunnit?'

'What on?'

'Your offer.' He was annoyed at Chris's offhand attitude and was beginning to show it. 'You get that toy for Christmas?' Arthur asked with an edge to his voice.

'Friend of mine – got to number five in the charts.'

'We get a lot of presents,' said Big John complacently.

'Only way to do business, isn't it?' replied Arthur confidently. 'Favours done – presents given. Then everybody's happy.'

Chris spun one of the stainless steel gadgets. 'OK,' he said in a brisk voice. 'You want the record companies here, you want booking agents, television, the musical press people. That takes a lot of arranging, you know. There are phone calls, drinks – that kind of thing.'

'All of that,' said Arthur vaguely.

'You'll need backing from top musicians, so that'll be three hundred for a start. Then there's my time, my staff's time, all the arrangements, the hassles, my reputation and joint management if I like her –' He paused for breath.

'Well, what does it add up to?' Arthur asked in a voice of doom.

'Six readies.'

'Well –' said Arthur beginning to try and beat him down. But Chris was quick to prevent him.

'No arguments, no haggling. Six hundred up front or that's it.' He paused. 'If she *is* a good chick singer you could end up making a fortune. It's the year of the chicks, everybody's saying that.'

Arthur forced a grandiose smile. 'Why else would I be interested? A man of my experience?'

That night found Arthur locked in a passionate clinch with Sharon in the front of his Jag. After a while, she gently disengaged herself.

'I'd better go now, Arthur.'

'Don't I get a cup of coffee?'

They were parked outside a house in a part of the Fulham Road that was still not classy.

'Oh, I'd really like to – but it's the other girls –'

'All right, darling, I understand. We'll soon have you out of this place, anyway.' He spoke confidently.

Sharon opened her eyes wide. 'Arthur, you've been so wonderful to me.'

'It's nothing,' he replied modestly.

'I mean – that Chinese meal. I never had nothing like that before.'

'Well, they know I like a good King Prawn in there.'

'And then going on to the Music Box. I mean that is really, really unbelievable.'

'Well – I told you – I'm well known, respected. You'll most likely end up with a record contract.' He adjusted his tie casually.

'No,' she gasped.

'Well, I've got a lot of record people coming down . . . most of them are personal acquaintances . . .'

Sharon threw her arms round him. 'Oh, Arthur –'

'When we get things sorted out, maybe we'll slip away for a few days. Been to Marbella?'

'It's all racing drivers down there, isn't it?'

'Sure – course, I know a few of them and all. James Hunt and Nicky what's-is-name.'

There was a short silence, then Sharon said, 'You know what we were saying earlier – 'bout the difference in ages and everything?'

'Yeah?' asked Arthur cautiously.

'I don't think it matters. I mean, all the stars do it, don't they? It's like they need a more mature man.'

'And you are a star, my darling,' said Arthur romantically sliding towards her. Quickly, Sharon gave him a peck on the cheek. Her hand was on the door handle.

'You won't get into trouble or nothing?'

'Sorry?'

'At home, I mean.'

A mental picture of 'er indoors swam into Arthur's mind. 'Sharon, my darling, I told you . . .' he said. 'I know how to handle everything.'

'That's good, Arthur,' she said as she slipped hurriedly out of the car.

Terry was in bed asleep when Arthur knocked on the door. He stirred, Arthur knocked again and Terry tumbled out of bed. He hitched on his Y-fronts and went to the door.

'Yeah?'

'Me.'

Wearily, Terry opened the door, switched on the light and admitted Arthur.

'What time is it?' asked Terry yawning.

Arthur glanced round the flat, taking in the fact that the place had not been cleaned for some time. He wrinkled his nose in disgust. 'Gawd almighty, you live in this filth? It's a quarter to five.'

'Late night or an early start?'

Terry went back to his bed and curled up, wishing that Arthur was just a nasty dream. But he wasn't – he was for real.

' 'Er indoors only locked me out, hasn't she?'

'Thought you had her well trained?'

'I gave Sharon a bell from home – must have been ear-molling on the extension.'

'Yeah, I seen the movie.'

Arthur scowled at Terry and brushed a few newspapers off the couch. 'Well, don't I get a cup of tea or nothing?'

'Only if you brought your own tea-bag.'

Arthur took off his jacket. 'You got a duvet or something?'

'There's a tartan travelling rug in the airing cupboard.'

'Where's that?'

'In the kitchen under the shelf with the marmalade.'

'Gawd. This is a carsie.'

Terry said sleepily, burying his head under the blankets, 'Next to the kitchen . . .'

Arthur scowled, went through to the kitchen and looked around for the rug, opening cupboards and making a great deal of noise.

'Simon come about those jeans?' asked Arthur poking his head into the bedroom area.

Terry was silent.

'Hey,' Arthur repeated loudly, 'Simon come about –'

Terry sat up, annoyed. 'Course he bloody well did. Said they was Albanian and also pointed out you spell Levi with an I not a Y.'

Arthur came back into the room, shaking the tartan rug.

'What they all got against Albania? They was on our side during the war.' He looked at the rug in horror. 'Hey, this has got stuff all over it.'

'I burst a bag of wheat germ over it.'

'Got every other kind of bleeding germ as well,' he muttered, taking off his trousers, folding them neatly and putting them over the back of the sofa. Then he sat down heavily. 'I might get a flat with that Sharon,' he pronounced.

'Hallo, young lovers wherever you are,' yawned Terry. 'Anyway, you been married twenty-eight years,' he said.

'Well – she got her cards tonight. I told her.'

'Thought she locked you out.'

'She did. I shouted through the letter box.' Arthur tried to settle on the sofa. 'This cushion could do with a visit to Sketchley's and all.'

But there was no response from Terry.

'Hey!'

'What?'

'Get me up at quarter to eight.'

'What for?'

'Well, I've got to get the kids to school, haven't I,' said Arthur petulantly.

'Oh yeah – I forgot that.'

'Forgot what?'

'If they don't turn up in a Jag, they get expelled, don't they?' Terry pulled the hanging light switch. 'Now, Arthur, why don't you get some kip?'

Well before the disco opened for business, Sharon was on stage with Barry's group. Whilst she waited, they were having a blow and producing some excellent rock and jazz.

But Sharon thought they were never going to end and when they eventually did, she wasn't in the best of moods.

'I don't suppose there would be the slightest chance of us rehearsing one of *my* numbers now, would there?'

Barry, the leader and keyboard-player, glanced up. 'Oh, sorry love. What d'you want to do?'

' "Who Can I Turn To?" ' she said flatly.

Barry paused. Clearly, he was not very familiar with the tune. 'Yeah – well, what key?' he asked vaguely.

'Well, I don't know, do I? You're the one who's supposed to know about things like that.'

'It's this one, isn't it?' He picked out the melody with one finger.

'Yeah, but it's too high – and I do it very slow.'

Barry stared at the keys for some time. Then he said,

'Okay – as the man said – you try it and we'll follow you.'
But already the lead guitar player was muttering, 'I won't. I've never even heard of it.'

Meanwhile, Arthur, looking much smarter than usual, was propping up the bar of the Winchester. Terry stood disconsolately beside him.

'What do you mean, "you don't fancy it"?' snapped Arthur.

'Well, it's not my scene is it? I don't like that kind of music.'

'Terence – have you forgotten I am launching a star?'

'Yeah, but you're not going to get riots down there, are you? You'll be doing all the glad-handling and that. There's no need for me.'

'I thought you might want to share in a moment of triumph,' said Arthur huffily.

Terry protested. 'I'm saying good luck and everything. But I've been doing that metrication all day – and I've got a meet with a bird at nine.'

'So bring her down.'

'I promised her a Greek meal.'

'So have a quick doner kebab and chips and bring her down.'

'She's into soul music. Look – I'll see how it goes.'

'Very considerate of you.'

Terry lowered his voice. 'By the way – the sofa tonight – probably not on. Know what I mean?'

'Did I ask?'

'No. But –'

'Hotels all over the place, y'know.'

'T'riffic. No problem.'

Arthur sipped his drink meditatively. 'And might I enquire – who is this little creature who makes you forsake your friends?'

Terry gave a modest shrug. 'Air hostess.'

'Oh, not the little blonde number?'

'Yeah.'

'Oh well, she's not exactly jet set, is she? Not – "I'm Penny . . . fly me to Dallas, Texas".' Arthur was enjoying being condescending, whilst secretly worrying where he was going to lay his head for the night if 'er indoors shut him out again.

'No. Her name's Rita and she's on the London-Manchester shuttle service.'

'She don't exactly need to be fluent in three languages for that, does she?' Arthur said sarcastically.

'No. But at least she don't sing,' said Terry quickly.

'Thank you, Terence,' replied Arthur. 'It's good to know who your friends are. Particularly when you need a little support.'

As Sharon wavered her way through "Who Can I Turn To", Arthur prowled the balcony area of the disco impatiently. She was wearing his dress and it was this additional expense, on top of everything else, that made him worried for there were only a dozen or so patrons in the whole place. Finally, Arthur went to the bar.

'Vodka and Slimline and where's all the people?'

'Monday night, innit. Anyway, most nights they don't come in till the boozers close,' said the barman.

Suddenly, Arthur spotted Big John. 'Oi.'

'Yeah?'

'Where are they?'

'Dunno.'

'The faces, the record producers – the guests?'

'Didn't show.'

He walked away, while Arthur glanced dismally over the balcony as Sharon finished her song – to no applause whatsoever. Arthur, outraged, turned to hear a young bloke say:

'They'll be doing Come Dancing next week . . .'

Arthur returned to the bar where his drink was waiting. 'Stick another vodka in there,' he told the barman desperately as Sharon said into the mike:

'Now I'd like to do a beautiful love song called "Shadow Of Your Smile".'

Barry turned to the band, glad that he could recognise the

tune. 'One and two and three and four . . .'

Raggedly and slightly apart – the band and Sharon began but then the worst happened and Sharon dried, whilst the band played on. She stared round the vast auditorium with its scattering of punters, tears running down her cheeks. For a moment Sharon stood there frozen, and then ran off the stage.

'Oh Gawd,' said Arthur, taking a long swig of vodka. He ran down the stairs whilst the DJ quickly spun a record and the disco filled with music that was clearly much more acceptable.

Once backstage, Arthur found Sharon sitting on a bench sobbing her heart out. Quickly, she put his arms round her.

'All right, darling – now don't you fret about anything.'

'They're pigs, Arthur . . . they're all pigs. They don't appreciate nothing,' she wept.

As Arthur tried to console her, Barry arrived.

'Sorry, Sharon, we just wasn't very much together.' He sounded genuinely apologetic, but Arthur was furious.

'You ought to get nicked with a band like that.'

'Wasn't our fault.' Barry was defensive now.

'Well, whose fault was it then?'

'She just hit a few bum notes.'

'Bum notes? Well, you're not exactly Mantovani, are you?'

'Who?'

' "Who?" he asks. Mantovani – a man who could play anything with a bloody big orchestra and all.'

'They're difficult sort of numbers for a group like ours.' He was once again apologetic and Arthur wagged an angry finger at him.

'Look – for three hundred a throw you should be able to get through the Warsaw Concerto –'

'For what?'

'Your bleeding fee,' said Arthur ungraciously.

Barry, however, looked totally bewildered. 'We got twenty-five quid between us and that's a fiver more than we got last time.'

Arthur stared at him, unbelieving. 'What'd you say?'

'Twenty-five.'

Arthur took out his silk handkerchief and threw it at Barry imperiously. As he hurried towards the stairs, he shouted, 'Dry her tears.'

Arthur was very much out of breath as he flung open Chris's office door and stood panting on the threshold. Chris was behind his big executive desk, with Big John sitting on the sofa. Both had large drinks in their hands as they stared at the enraged Arthur, who said in a measured voice, 'You've turned me over, you –' He advanced a few tottering paces.

'Just calm down, Mister Daley,' said Chris casually.

'Calm down? Six hundred you've had off me –'

'She went on. She went off. Not my fault.' He shrugged as if to finalise the whole business.

'And the people? All the celebs? The record producers?' Arthur's voice spluttered and died away as he leant on the desk for support, badly out of breath.

'They didn't show. Invites, telephone calls. Did I try my best, John?'

'Fingers to the bone, we worked,' said Big John grinning.

'You're lying.'

'That's nice,' said Big John.

'I want my dough back,' yelled Arthur.

Chris spoke slowly and carefully. 'All I can suggest is that you put the matter in the hands of your legal advisers.'

'I don't have legal advisers. I have people who come round and punch your head in,' said Arthur threateningly.

Slowly, Big John levered himself up from the sofa and placed a meaty hand on Arthur's shoulder. 'Mister Daley. That is a very nasty threat –'

'Made in front of witnesses,' said Chris officiously. 'Perhaps you'd show Mister Daley to the door, John?'

Big John squeezed Arthur's elbow with less than loving concern.

'That is a two hundred pounds suit,' protested Arthur.

'Then we don't want to get it all messed up, do we?' replied Big John, still holding Arthur's elbow, now in a grip of iron.

'You don't know me, do you?' said Arthur with attempted dignity.

'We have heard the name,' replied Chris reflectively. 'What was that old election slogan? "Yesterday's people." That's the trouble, Mister Daley – times change. See you, eh?'

Big John led Arthur to the door and it was only when he was in the corridor that Arthur found the strength to say, 'Up yours.' But by that time the office door was closed and, anyway, Arthur's voice was very soft.

Terry was sorting out some shirts in the lock-up next morning, trying to arrange them in neat piles. From time to time he jotted down a calculation in a notebook.

'So that's . . . one inch equals two and a half centimetres and a bit. And that's two and a half into forty is . . . erm . . .' he was saying somewhat desperately to himself as an enraged Arthur blew in. 'I think I cracked this metrication –'

'Yeah? Well, forget it.'

'What? After all –'

'They had me over, Terry.'

Terry's indignation turned to smiles. 'No Stars on Sunday?'

'That Chris is going to be seeing a few stars.' He glanced at one of the shirts. 'Forty – that's a seventeen collar, near enough.'

'Oh, nice –' said Terry, 'I thought it was the chest size.'

But Arthur's anger continued to mount as he recalled the humiliating events of the previous evening. 'They tucked me up very nice with a bleeding awful band. As to producers and record execs – they had about ten squatters in the place sharing a half pint of shandy between them.'

'That's show business, Arthur.'

'That's a diabolical business. Six hundred sovs. That little flash Chris stole my money. And that, my son, is a crime – a liberty. So you forget about metrication and go down there and give him a pull.'

'Get the money back?'

'Right.'

'And suppose he don't want to pay?'

'Then he gets a spank. And he keeps getting spanked till he does want to pay.'

'Hmm,' said Terry derisively.

'What d'you mean "hmm"?'

'I mean them days are over.'

'What?'

'Putting the frighteners on people. Doing favours for guys. Collecting bad gambling debts – it's all gone, like the Blue Gardenia.'

'What do you mean – gambling debts! This man *stole* from me.'

'He ripped you off – and that's *your* game. How many mug punters have you had over? You thought you was on a good thing with Fulham's answer to Tina Turner and you backed a loser. All right – tough.'

'He threatened me.'

'What was he going to do? Hit you with his silver bracelet?'

Arthur shook his head and walked restlessly round the storeroom, occasionally shooting an angry glance at Terry. 'This is marvellous, innit? I mean, you are supposed to mind out for me. And here I am with a genuine grievance and you don't want to know. How's that going to sound around the manor? What does that do for my image?'

'What image?'

'Listen, sunshine. I am a highly respected person –'

'And where would that be – "sunshine". A few afternoon drinking clubs? Car auctions? A few old villains with long memories?'

Arthur gave Terry a long, hurt look. 'I don't know what's got into you. I mean, have I done you a favour or three?'

'Four even.'

'Looked after your Mum when you were away?'

'Sure.'

'Dropped round with a few prezzies?'

'Nice set of dralon curtains as advertised on Police Five – she wouldn't be without them.'

Arthur gave Terry a tolerant smile. 'Set you up when you came out?'

'You're getting there, Arthur. Now you're setting me up to go back inside.'

'I'm asking you to return a few favours,' said Arthur patiently.

'I'm doing that right now – in metric an' all.' He waved a shirt under Arthur's nose. 'What's a thirty-six?'

'Fifteen, fifteen and a half – I dunno. Won't do your reputation any good either.'

'Well it might do with the prison after-care service.'

'I am not asking you to go and shoot the geezer. Just a bit of friendly retribution.'

'That's not my game and you know it, Arthur.'

'Well, what is, I wonder?' He put in unpleasantly. 'Certainly not conversion tables. The man has nicked six hundred out of my pocket and what you're saying is I should stand for that, eh?'

Terry scowled as he tossed a bundle of shirts across the table. 'No, I'm not.'

'Well, what then?'

'I dunno. Solicitor's letter. I mean, six hundred – that's high finance, innit?'

Arthur was so disgusted that he lit a Panatella. 'Just sussed it – bottle job. That it? Happens. You've said it yourself in the past – "always going to be somebody better". Now it has come to pass,' Arthur paused for effect. 'That Chris is well protected so you've made your decision. Swallowed it.'

'Look.' Terry held up his hand. 'Trembling, eh? The guy he's got down there – I'd have him over in ten seconds, including the count.'

'Course you would,' replied Arthur, pausing for effect. 'Then you give that little Chris a whack and walk out with the money – and you get a nice drink out of it.'

'And Chris calls the Old Bill and I'm up on assault, demanding money with menaces. Haven't you got it yet, Arthur? I'm not doing it. End of message . . . right?' His tone was final, decisive and his message received a stony look from Arthur.

'Right – end of job and all.'

Terry looked at him for a moment, suddenly realising that, for once, Arthur meant what he was saying. 'Obviously, redundancy money is out of the question –' He pocketed the notebook and pen, but Arthur was too quick for him.

'My biro and notebook,' he said coldly.

Terry, headed for the door, flinging the biro and notebook in the direction of the workbench. 'Yeah – I'd hate to get caught ripping you off for a biro and a notebook. I mean – you might put a contract out on me.' He slammed the door behind him, leaving Arthur staring after him.

When a disgruntled, very upset Arthur phoned, Sharon was in bed with Barry. This, however, was something she did not confide in her impressario, as she put her finger to her lips whilst Arthur spoke reassuringly into the phone.

'Hallo, my love . . . how are you . . ?'

'As well as anyone could expect after last night,' she complained.

'Don't you worry about it. We'll get something together. Mebbe we'll have a bit of a meal tonight . . . eh?'

'Don't really know that I can tonight, Arthur –'

'Why not?'

'I was going to rehearse, see.'

'Where?'

'Not sure. You know Barry? The keyboard player.'

'Barry?'

'He's going to teach me all about chromatic scales and that.'

'But he was diabolical.'

Barry waved a clenched fist towards the phone, but Sharon again put her finger to her lips.

'No – he's good. He really is. And he's a good contact. See, last night wasn't his fault. Tell you what – can you phone me later? And I'll tell you where I'm going to be. You know – I'm thinking of doing a whole new act.'

'Whole new act? All right, my love, don't you worry. I'll call you later. Bye.'

'Byyyee.'

She hung up and turned back to Barry.

'He's a right creep,' said Barry.

'He's been like a dad to me,' reproved Sharon.

'More like a sugar-dad.' Barry took her in his arms.

Terry returned to his flat depressed, angry and equally as upset as Arthur at their parting. But once inside, he was amazed to find that the familiar tip had become a clean, sparkling little palace. Then with a rush of pleasure, Terry saw his air hostess girl-friend walking out of the kitchen.

'Thought you were working?' she said in the Northern accent that he loved.

'Penny, love – you do all this?' he said delightedly.

'Well, you can't say it didn't need it.'

'I think I'd better have you living in.' He took her in his arms.

After a while, she said, 'You're spoiling my uniform. I've got to look fresh and alluring for all those fellers who want to fly me to sun-drenched Manchester. Where have you been?'

'Having a row with Arthur,' said Terry, flopping into a chair.

Penny looked surprised. 'Your best friend? Great pal . . . man who's like a dad to you?'

'Yeah – well he wanted a favour that could land me back somewhere I haven't been for a good few years.'

'Then don't do it.' She gave him a quick kiss on the cheek. 'I'd miss you.'

Terry sighed. 'But a pal is a pal is a pal –' He broke off, staring into space.

'Somebody hurt him?'

'Only where he feels it most – in his pocket.'

'Look, pardon the expression, but I've got to fly. I've got three days off in eight days' time and I thought I'd spend it in London. We could have a lot of fun if you're not in Wormwood Scrubs. And I'll tell you another thing –'

'You love me, right?' asked Terry grinning.

'Yeah – but get some new bags for your vacuum cleaner.'

When she had gone, Terry leant back in the chair. After a moment he got up, glanced in the mirror and patted his hair.

'Know what you are, son? You're a right old charmer,' he said to himself.

Then Arthur's face swam into his mind and he winced.

In the Winchester Club that afternoon, Arthur was off-loading his troubles on to a sympathetic Dave.

'To tell you the truth, Arthur, I'm sorry to hear it,' Dave said.

'It happens,' Arthur replied gloomily. ' "Foresake not an old friend", as the good book has it. And that's what he's done.' Then he said quickly. 'Dave – I'm not asking you to take sides. All I'm saying is that if Terry'd been where he should've been it would never've happened. I was heavily outnumbered. Outgunned, you might say.'

Dave lowered his voice. 'They had shooters out?'

'Figuratively. I'll put it no stronger than that.'

The doorbell of the club rang and Dave turned to a slim, elderly man who sometimes acted as a helper. 'Get that, Jimmy.' Dave turned to Arthur. 'Squeeze another one in there, Arthur?'

Arthur's glass was full, but he quickly took a couple of sips. 'Why not?' he said recklessly.

Jimmy reappeared alone, looking worried. 'It's Vic Piner.'

'Well, just leave the door closed.'

'Says he's got a meet with Arthur –'

'Yeah, that's right.'

'Leave it out, Arthur,' said Dave sharply. 'The man's barred.'

'He'll be in my company. I'll vouch for him – all right?'

'You're joking.'

'We're going to discuss a little business.'

'Sorry. Not here. No offence to you, but the man has upset too many people. He don't come in and that's it.' Dave's voice, for once, was absolutely definite.

'Well, I'm certainly learning something about friends today,' he said bitterly. 'Cheers.' Arthur drained his glass and headed for the door. Behind him Dave raised his eyebrows at Jimmy. Arthur was in deep water.

Vic Piner leant against Arthur's Jag which was parked just outside the Winchester Club. Vic looked like what he was – a thug, a bully and a nutter. There was also an aura of evil about him which Arthur detected all too well.

'You're not all that popular, Vic.'

He became immediately aggressive. 'He slag me off, that Dave?'

'Take it easy,' said Arthur quickly. 'Just said you were barred. He cast no aspersions upon you in person. I think we'll have to have a cup of tea somewhere.'

Arthur got into his Jag, opened the passenger door for Vic and waited for the reaction.

'Tea?' asked Vic in a voice of awe.

'Well, are there any licensed premises in the manor where you're not barred?'

Vic shrugged and clambered into his seat. 'No,' he said.

'Wonder why?' asked Arthur innocently as he drove off.

'I get picked on a lot,' said Vic by way of explanation. 'People look at me and say "Who's he think he is?" So I tell 'em. My brother is the same. So you got to stand by 'em ain't you? I mean – family and all.'

'Oh yes,' remarked Arthur. 'The family's a very precious thing.'

'You want some geezer done over, do you?' Vic came straight to the point.

'Just persuaded to pay a little debt.'

'Drop by my brother's yard then,' said Vic invitingly.

Arthur hesitated. 'I don't think it needs the whole family Piner.'

But Vic seemed impatient to be family minded. 'It's only round the corner,' he said. 'Let's drop by.'

Apprehensively, knowing he was getting further and further into something he couldn't control, Arthur drove to the Piners' scrapyard. Then they both got out of the car, Arthur reluctantly, and began to walk towards a shed at the end of the yard.

Vic's brother, Henry, was bigger and more vicious looking than Vic – if that were possible.

'Henry,' said Vic enthusiastically. 'Show Arthur your collection.' Henry looked pleased and pushed a couple of cabinets aside to reveal a trapdoor. Opening it he displayed a collection of weapons which included bayonets, swords, two sawn-off shotguns and a couple of dockers' hoods. Vic reached down lovingly. 'That's an antique, innit – Austin Seven starting handle. And this –' he pulled at a gleaming bayonet – 'World War One that is,' said Vic in hallowed tones.

'I keep 'em nice,' remarked Henry, as if he was talking about a stamp collection.

'They – they all been used?' asked Arthur looking worried.

'Oh yeah. Like depending how much you want to hurt 'em,' Vic said in a matter of fact voice.

'Yeah, but any one of these things could kill somebody,' pursued Arthur, sweat breaking out on his brow.

'Easy,' replied Henry.

'I don't want anybody killed – just frightened a bit,' pleaded Arthur.

'Well – you tell him you're going to kill him, that'll frighten him, won't it?' said Vic logically.

'He only owes me six hundred.'

Vic paused. 'Let's say he only owes you three hundred now. See what I mean?'

Arthur gave Vic the bleakest of smiles for he could see only too well what he meant.

Whilst Arthur was getting into a situation he couldn't handle, Terry and Dave were having an urgent whispered conference in the Winchester.

'You don't tell him I told you though. You don't say I phoned. But that Vic – they wouldn't even fancy him in Broadmoor,' Dave told him.

'OK, but Arthur's over twenty-one. He's made his decision.'

'Terry – your old pal could be up on a murder conspiracy charge.'

There was a long silence during which Terry thought deeply. Then Terry said, 'You ought to've heard the birds sing an' all . . .'

Once Terry had made up his mind, he acted fast. Arriving at the disco entrance, he quickly looked up and down the street, hoping to see Arthur's Jag. But there was no sign. As Terry hesitated, Big John opened the disco doors and spotted him. He spoke ungraciously. 'What the hell do you want?'

'Anybody called to see you, guv'nor?'

'What's it to you?'

'What's it to *you* more like it –'

He brushed past Big John, who made a grab for him. But he neatly side-stepped and slammed Big John up against a wall.

'Now listen – I'm doing you a favour. You keep these doors shut, right, 'cause you've got a lot of trouble heading this way and you want to be well clear when it arrives. In other words – lock 'em.'

Such was the note of real urgency in Terry's voice that Big John hurriedly closed the doors.

'Where's what's-'is-name – Chris?'

'Up there.' He pointed to the stairs. 'Oi,' he said as Terry disappeared up them. Lumberingly, he followed only to discover Terry confronting Chris in the middle of his electric shave.

'Right, now listen –'

Startled, Chris backed away and began to shout for Big John.

'Never mind John. You're gonna need half the Airborne Division if you don't listen to me.'

Chris then saw that Big John was at the door, but was making no attempt to tackle Terry.

Seizing his opportunity, Terry began to bash his point

home. 'You had Arthur Daley over –'

'It was his own fault.'

'All right. Good luck. Now Arthur's a bit tight with his money as you may have noticed.'

'If you've come in here threatening me –'

'Shurrup. Heard of Vic Piner?'

There was a blank look from Chris, but Big John nodded sagely.

'Well, muscles has heard of him. He's a nutter. Mad Vic – not vapour rub. This guy gets on your chest and he stays there, and you'll need more'n that St Christopher medallion to get you home safe.'

'He's right, Chris,' said Big John looking uneasy.

'What's he going to do then?' asked Chris reluctantly.

'He's gonna take the money and then give you a hiding just for the fun of it.'

'And what's your angle?'

'Oh, you're one of them, eh? Everybody's got to have an angle? Well, mine's simple – Arthur's an old pal and I can't afford the petrol to go and see him wherever they lock him up. And second – I don't see why you should get your legs broken for being a bit too greedy.'

Then they all froze as a determined banging suddenly began on the front door.

'Oh, Christ,' said Big John, 'this is it.'

'Not if you keep your cool,' said Terry. He ran lightly out of the office, hurried down the stairs, listened and then heard a movement in the auditorium. Tiptoeing inside he saw, under a few working lights, dim shadows of Arthur and Vic crossing the auditorium towards the main staircase. Deliberately, Terry cleared his throat and they turned abruptly to face him.

'Bit early for the dancing, aren't you?' he said smiling, beginning to walk towards them.

'What you doing here?' asked Arthur with hostility.

'Chatting with my old pal, Chris, who tenders his apologies and says you left this behind in his office.' He tossed a neatly taped bundle of notes over to the astonished

Arthur. 'Four hundred. He reckons he was due a twoer just to teach you a lesson and putting up with hearing the bird sing. Fair?'

'Reasonable,' said Arthur.

'Of course it's been a wasted journey for poor old Vic here.'

Vic glared at Terry, maniacally enraged. Arthur began to back off.

'You just nicked my job –' spluttered Vic.

'Job? You're not even on the firm.'

'I was on three hundred.'

'What's that? Hundred a year?'

At that point Vic went crazy. 'Bastard!' he yelled and dived at Terry. But Terry simply wasn't there. Vic moved again. They grappled, fell against the console and the lights began to flash, a tape of rock music automatically played, drowning Vic's heavy breathing. So far, he hadn't landed a punch and Terry was handling him with ease. Arthur watched with cautious admiration.

Terry suddenly broke the clinch, pushed Vic back and hit him on the chin. He thudded to the floor and stayed there.

'Arthur, I'm surprised at you. I always thought you was a good judge of a fighter,' Terry said as they both stared down at the prone figure of Vic.

Arthur nodded and smiled wryly. 'Yeah,' he said.

Terry then crossed to the fallen Vic and knelt over him, bringing him back to consciousness with a few face slaps. Vic stared at him muzzily.

'Hear all right?' asked Terry.

'Yeah,' he said, wincing with the pain.

'I'll do a deal with you. You and your brother don't start a war and I won't tell a soul that it only took one good right hand to knock you spark out. OK?'

Vic nodded unhappily.

'Together,' said Arthur, 'we're very clever.' They were driving towards the lock-up in Arthur's Jag, with Arthur triumphantly at the wheel.

'Putting mad Vic onto him, that wasn't too clever, was it?'

'Wasn't it?' said Arthur vaguely.

'Well, was it?' demanded Terry.

'Soon got you working, didn't it?' he replied truculently. Then Arthur saw something that he didn't like. 'Oh, my Gawd.'

Once again a police car was outside the lock-up, but this time the big wooden doors were wide open. Detective Sergeant Chisholm was waiting as Arthur hurried agitatedly from the car and Terry followed more casually.

'Did you this time, Arthur. Cleared you out,' said Chisholm cheerfully.

Arthur glanced into the empty storeroom with an expression of acute loss on his face. Then, instantly, he recovered his ability to bluff. 'Nothing in it anyway,' he said airily.

'Nothing?' asked Chisholm.

'Just a few odds and ends – that's all.'

'All we found was a few records – musical that is, not criminal.' He laughed quietly at his own joke.

'Well, Arthur's very partial to a bit of music,' said Terry.

'Matter of fact, Mister Chisholm, I used to be in the business. Managing a girl singer.'

'What happened to her?' asked Chisholm.

'Well, you know – kids these days. She ran off with a tone-deaf piano player.'

Arthur walked into the storeroom with Terry following, pausing only to make a weary gesture of resignation to Chisholm. 'That's show business, Mister Chisholm,' he said.

PART THREE

Following their rift, Arthur had decided to behave so generously towards Terry that they both found it completely exhausting. Eventually, Dave couldn't stand it any longer as they slapped each other's backs in the Winchester.

'When are you two love-birds gonna stop cooing?' he asked hopefully.

'What do you want?' asked Terry. 'Blood?'

'You don't understand, Dave,' said Arthur. 'You've never experienced true bonding.'

'True what, Arthur?'

'Bonding, Dave. Together we're a team. Apart we're rubbish. Isn't that so, Terry?'

'Yes, Arthur.' It was strange to have Arthur so compliant, so generous. He was waiting for the bubble to burst so that they could return to their old relationship. But Arthur was still so pleased to get his money back that it was as if he had sworn eternal friendship. It was all a bit wearing.

'You see, Dave,' said Arthur, waxing philosophical. 'A true partnership gives and never minds the cost.'

'Eh?'

'And when in doubt, turns inwards, seeking strength. Then it's out to conquer the evening. See what I mean?'

'It's truly wonderful,' said Dave.

'Ah – you can mock. But you cannot break our glass walls with your stones. We are invincible. And what about another Dave? Fill 'em up and let's drink to the team.'

'You're very silent, Terry,' said Dave as he poured vodka for Arthur and lager for Terry.

'I was just basking in the warmth of it all,' he said. 'Getting a tan in the sun that shines out of Arthur's – whole being.'

Arthur smiled benignly. 'And we can share a joke, too.'

Dave asked, 'So all this minder business is out of the window, is it?'

Arthur looked perturbed. 'You're speaking in riddles,' he said. 'I'm a simple cove.'

'Yeah – what I mean is – you're equal partners now, are you?'

Arthur paused, reflecting on the beauty of it all. 'Terry

still looks out for me – he's the younger man.'

'You share and share alike?'

'I give him part of my crust.' Arthur looked at his watch. 'I must be toddling off.'

'Got some business to do, Arthur?' asked Dave.

'I'm a busy man.'

'Not got another chick who's gonna be a pop star?' Dave's face creased into the suggestion of a smile. Terry grinned, but Arthur frowned.

'That's in poor taste – don't take the piss out of my benevolence,' he remonstrated.

'Sorry, Arthur.'

'Where you going?' asked Terry.

'Bit of business in Southall.' Arthur downed the last of his vodka.

'You didn't tell me about that.'

'Just needs a bit of preliminary reconnaissance,' He hurried out of the bar.

When Arthur had gone Dave said to Terry, 'That'll be a tenner for the drinks.'

Terry froze and then his hand went reluctantly to his pocket.

'All in the spirit of true friendship,' said Dave happily.

Southall seemed the lively centre of a new Bombay. Greengrocery shops spilled on to the pavement, butchers' shops had meat on one side and video tapes on the other and the gift shops had windows bursting with gaudy Indian jewellery. There were Indian banks, cafés, restaurants and a smell of spice overlaid the petrol and diesel fumes of the passing traffic and the blander aroma of fish and chips and hamburgers.

Arthur parked his Jag and began to look for an address. A stranger in a strange land, he was uncomfortable – and would have been much happier walking down Fulham Broadway. But he plodded on, passing a Sikh reading an Indian newspaper on the street corner.

Then Arthur recognised the address he had been

searching for – a radio, TV and video shop. Walking cautiously inside, Arthur faced the owner – an elderly Hindu. Suffering from the cold, he wore mittens, a long scarf and a Husky waistcoat. His English was shaky and he gave Arthur a deeply suspicious look, partly because he had met him once before and also because he was deeply suspicious anyway. Life in England seemed far more devious than life in India and, to Ajit, Arthur seemed to be the very epitome of deviousness.

'All right, guv'nor? Shamy about?'

'No.'

'Is he coming back?'

'Don't know.'

Arthur looked at a TV monitor set showing an Indian film. 'Nice, eh? You remember me – Mister Daley?'

'Yes.'

'We met once before.'

'Yes.'

Arthur paused. Did he detect a lack of communication? Then he said, 'I've got a meet with Shamy.'

'Yes.'

'Well, where is he?' he asked with an edge of impatience.

'Not here.'

'I've got that. He's not here. Let's start again.'

'Shamy running.'

'Yeah, I know he's a bit slippery. But where? Home? The bank? Betting shop? Boozer? –'

Ajit pointed to the street.

'Running – out there?' asked Arthur.

Ajit hesitated, locked the till and then shepherded Arthur to the door. 'There.'

Arthur looked down the street. 'Gone for a cup of tea?'

'Tea?'

'Thank you kindly.' He nodded at the till. 'Don't get cold, you get back to the old Jack and Jill.' Arthur then began to hurry down the street towards an Indian cafeteria.

Walking in, he made the predictable discovery that all the customers were Asians. At a corner table sat Shamy. He was in his late twenties, casually dressed, handsome and full of confidence. Directly his eyes fell on Arthur, he gave a start of annoyance. Then his features rearranged themselves into a warm smile. Shamy stood up and shook Arthur by the hand.

'Arthur – nice to see you.' He turned to the owner of the cafe. 'Rajiv – a cup of tea for Mister Daley, please.'

'The old feller said you was running.'

'You know me, Arthur. Busy, busy. I've got things to do.'

'It's your shop, is it?'

'Yeah, more or less,' he said uneasily. 'The old bloke, he's just a peasant. He can hardly speak English. What does he know about hi-fi and videos? He had two goats and a field of of rice in the old country and he's still got the peasant mentality. Shrewd, mind you. A lot of them are like that. He'll probably be a millionaire in a couple of years.'

'Talking about millionaires,' said Arthur slowly.

'I know what you're going to say and I've got it. OK?' Shamy gave a quick, wary glance around him. Then he fished out a wad of twenty-pound notes. 'Monkey, right? You did me a right favour. Those reconditioned sewing machines were a real winner.'

'The old values,' said Arthur nostalgically. 'They don't want to know about home-made dresses in this country. Young wives – they want coffee mornings with their Tupperware, but they can't even darn a sock. Your womenfolk have got their priorities right. I couldn't sell those sewing machines in Fulham.'

The waiter brought them a cup of tea as Arthur pontificated. 'They hardly know how to thread a needle and some of them can't even thaw a couple of fish cakes. How's your good lady these days?'

'Still working at Charlie Chester's Casino. She's doing roulette and blackjack now.'

'Nice.' He paused. 'She'll probably leave now that you're doing well.'

'I don't know about that, Arthur –'

'Don't be modest. I've known you for a few years. What can I say about you – a ne'er-do-well? Could I go farther? A tea-leaf? A drunkard? A gambler, a cheat, a sponger and you were prone to make up pork pies, as well. Oh yes, you were an all-round ponce, sure enough.'

Shamy looked a little disappointed. 'Well, nobody's perfect, are they?'

'I know what's happened? You're back with your own folk – you're at home.' Arthur looked delighted with this little piece of wisdom and he gave Shamy a sickly smile.

'I'm just a Londoner,' shrugged Shamy.

'You may think so, but all that dashing around the West End doing the Find the Lady, living in Whitechapel – that wasn't *you*.'

'The only reason I left was because the Bill gave me a lot of aggro and I got mugged three times – 'cause they thought I was a Paki.' He spread his hands. 'What could I do?'

'Well, you won't have that here, will you?' Arthur sipped his tea. 'And they make a nice cup of tea as well. I'm proud of you, Shamy.'

'Thank you – that's real praise. Incidentally, have you got any video machines?'

'Well –'

'Do you know anything about that game?'

Arthur laughed patiently. 'Do I? I was a pioneer, wasn't I? I've still got two tapes of "Dixon of Dock Green" – that's how long I've been in that area. Are you expanding?'

'Indians do love a film.'

'I've heard that,' said Arthur, shaking his head wisely.

'They make more films in India than in Hollywood.'

'You surprise me –'

'They'd rather have a video than an Oxfam parcel.'

Arthur stared at him. 'You *have* changed, haven't you? What you've got now is imagination – a world view.'

'Ambition – that's what it is.'

'It's nice to hear that.'

'Nobody makes money by working –'

'Ah,' said Arthur, 'that's where you're wrong, see. Look at your compatriots with their little newsagent shops.'

'Yeah, I have,' said Shamy. What do they get after twenty

years? A lot of old newspapers – that's what.' He smiled sadly across the table.

One phrase blazed across Arthur's mind – he's got it sussed.

As Arthur came out of the café, he noticed that an Indian traffic warden was sticking a parking ticket on the windscreen of his Jag.

'And a poppadum to you, darling,' muttered Arthur, but the traffic warden ignored him as she crossed to the other side of the street.

Inside a betting shop in Fulham, Terry was waiting for the girl settler to count out a winning bet.

'Five hundred and twenty-four. Who's a lucky boy then?'

'No luck in it, it's skill,' said Terry. 'Cheers.' Delightedly, Terry turned away from the counter. As he did so, he stuffed the money into his pocket and almost bumped into another punter who was wearing the worst wig in the world.

'Blimey,' said Terry. 'If it isn't Syrup.'* The middle-aged Syrup's wig was a grim travesty of the hair-style of Englebert Humperdink.

'Was that Arthur's winnings?' he asked.

'No . . . mine.'

'Handy.'

'Yeah. My first yankee –'

'I done hundreds of them.'

'Me too – but this is the first I've won.'

Syrup paused. 'I've done me lot.'

'There you go. And I know what you're going to say next.'

'No, I wasn't. You wouldn't like to sub me till tomorrow?'

'Well, what's happening tomorrow?' asked Terry dubiously.

'I don't know,' admitted Syrup.

'I'll give you a fiver.'

'Make it a score, eh?'

Terry hesitated.

*Syrup – syrup of figs – wig.

'I wanted to get some things. Bread and milk and some sweets for my little girl –'

'She's about twenty-nine,' Terry reminded him.

Syrup looked offended. 'Well, she still likes sweets, don't she?'

Terry palmed him a twenty pound note. 'Don't spend it all in one shop,' he said.

'You're a very generous man.'

'I know that,' said Terry briskly, but Syrup still wanted to talk.

'Gonna share you winnings with your mate Arthur, then?'

Terry looked at him in amazement. 'I wouldn't share a tent with Arthur.'

Ajit was studying a document given to him by a Mr Mitra, who was soberly dressed and looked like a bland accountant, when Shamy entered. Ajit looked up belligerently.

'Sorry I'm a bit late –'

'You go,' said Ajit.

'What's the matter?'

'Go . . . go.'

'Why?'

Mitra intervened, looking officious. 'Mister Desai has dispensed of your services.'

'Who are you then?'

'I'm his financial adviser and I've just advised him that you're too expensive. You want to be a partner, not an employee, don't you?'

Ajit suddenly lunged at Shamy, shouting, 'Thief, bloody thief.'

Shamy fended off the blow, muttering, 'He's a nutter.'

Mitra tried to calm Ajit and then said, 'You've been trying to dip in the till.'

'No chance. He's always got the key in his pocket.' But now Shamy's temper and sense of injustice was rising. 'I've helped him. Brought him lots of customers –'

'He wanted to call the police. There are many things missing,' said Mitra in schoolmasterly tones.

'Shoplifters.'

'Yes, and they're all your friends. It was you suggested that he should accept cheques and many have bounced – your friends again.' Mitra paused to let his censorious comments sink in. 'You took deposits on two TV sets and a music centre and the addresses are false.'

'It could happen to any shop.'

'Fifteen video tapes are missing.' He was almost intoning the list of offences now.

'He doesn't organise things. Anyway, he's a crook. He pirates tapes.'

'That is a very serious accusation. You must go.'

'Any chance of having my wages?' asked Shamy innocently.

Ajit moved purposefully towards him again and Shamy backed off.

'No wages – you had my money,' said Ajit, fighting for control.

'Yeah, well you might have given me money – but you gave no peace of mind.' He backed away to the door. 'You know what your problem is, don't you?' Shamy said to Ajit. 'You're a peasant – that's your problem.' He opened the door. 'You may have a BMW – but your brain is back with a bullock cart and a handful of patna rice. Cheers.' Shamy slammed the door, leaving Mitra to pour soothing words of comfort into Ajit's ears.

Back in the Winchester, Arthur was in his usual corner, holding forth with a magisterial account of his journey to darkest Southall. Terry sat beside him, while Dave served drinks. Across the bar sat Detective Sergeant Chisholm, listening quietly, but pretending to read his newspaper. Next to Terry sat Syrup, looking weirder than ever in his badly fitting wig.

'You see,' lectured Arthur, 'your Indian likes to graft. Up in the early morning to open his paper shop. Gets the kids off to school. Still open at 10 p.m. more than likely. You ought to have a look at Southall; it's a thriving place. Mind you, there's thousands of 'em. Brown faces – it's unnerving, you know. I only saw one white face and I think he was Richard Attenborough.' He turned to Dave. 'And one for yourself, Dave.'

Terry sat there worrying – was Arthur going to do the disappearing trick again, leaving him to pay? He knew he had to be on his guard or all his winnings would quickly disappear.

Dave nodded and glanced at Chisholm, wondering if he should be included in the round. Arthur shook his head quickly.

'I seen an Indian playing the bagpipes – years ago,' said Syrup.

'And?' asked Terry.

'You wouldn't think they'd bother.'

'Give one to the Syrup,' said Arthur unwillingly, anxious to return to the subject. 'You see, your friend and my friend – old Shamy – he's even got the flavour of hard work. Dashing around like a good 'un –'

'I don't believe it,' said Terry.

'I met him once. He was going down the hospital. They were going to X-ray him, just to see if he had a day's work about his person. Two pounds seventy, Arthur.'

With relief, Terry saw Arthur reaching for his wallet. 'He was dead worried when they brought in the three-day week. He thought it was compulsory –'

'You may scoff – but he's a different man now,' said Arthur with confidence, pulling out a twenty pound note and giving it to Dave. 'He's got incentives now. Just shows you, you *can* change a leopard's stripes –'

'You don't spot too many of them, do you,' said Terry drily, but Arthur ignored him.

Meanwhile, Dave was inspecting the twenty pound note, putting it up to the light and pursing his lips.

'I put it down to marriage,' continued Arthur oblivious to Dave's activities.

'He only married her because she had a steady job.'

'What a cynical man you are,' said Arthur, attacking him

for the first time in days. 'Just because your personal relationships are based on the physical rather than the spiritual, do not mock the state of matrimony. He's become a better man.'

Just as Terry was about to tell him why he hadn't, Dave interrupted. 'Could I have a word?' he said to Arthur, holding up the twenty pound note.

As he did so, Chisholm looked up, suddenly interested.

'It's not a wind-up, is it?' asked Dave humbly of Arthur.

'Eh?'

'If I didn't know you better –' Dave paused. 'I may have to rephrase that, Arthur. You wouldn't do this to an old friend? You wouldn't, would you?' He ended on a pleading note.

'Do what?'

'Just tell me that you didn't do it? Have a butchers.' Dave was becoming emotional.

Arthur grabbed the note and examined it against the light. 'I don't believe it.'

'You'd better. It's phoney as a glass eye.'

Arthur winced and his eyes darkened with disappointment and anger. He muttered to himself, 'He's done me up like a kipper.'

'Who?' asked Terry solicitously.

Then Arthur froze, realising that Chisholm was hovering like a hawk ready to pounce on a field mouse.

'Never mind,' said Arthur quickly.

'It's time I was moving on. I'll settle with you later, Dave.'

'Eh – will you, Arthur? Right.'

But Arthur's ruse was too late and Chisholm was amongst them. 'Do we have a little problem, Guv'nor?' he asked Dave.

'Not really, Mister Chisholm,' replied Dave uncomfortably, whilst Chisholm moved nearer to Arthur.

'I trust the bold Arthur Daley is not passing off counterfeit currency?'

'Me? Would I do a thing like that?'

'You don't want me to answer that, do you? May I?' He offered his hand to accept the note. Arthur gave the note to Dave, who passed it to Chisholm. The whole process was becoming a bit like a game in a children's play. At the same time, Arthur surreptitiously pulled out a wad of twenty pound notes and palmed them to Terry who palmed them to the Syrup.

'A fine piece of work, this,' said Chisholm having finished his examination. 'Any more where that came from, Arthur?'

'I didn't even know I had that one, Mister Chisholm. Some of these villains – I don't know.'

'I'm in a bit of a quandary. Obviously, you've broken the law.'

'I haven't lodged a complaint, Sergeant.'

'But I'm a witness – and I've got the evidence.'

'Yeah – but I didn't know it was bent.'

'All I know is that there are thousands of them in London. Ignorance of the law is no excuse – you know that – of all *people*. I think I'll have to nick you.' He moved nearer to Arthur, a sardonic smile on his face.

Arthur looked desperate and gabbled, 'Mister Chisholm – be fair. I'm a victim of circumstances. I've been turned over by some nasty little villain who has exploited my gullibility.'

'Where did you get it?'

'Ooh, I don't know. I'm a businessman. Money goes through my hands hour by hour.'

'Me too – sometimes. Incidentally, you still owe me two pounds seventy, Arthur,' put in Dave, anxious not to lose out.

'Dave – please. This is a crisis,' reprimanded Arthur.

'Yeah, I know – I'm out of pocket,' he said.

'In the book –'

Dave began to moan, whilst Chisholm looked on with the pleasure he took from other people's conflict. 'That bloody book is getting bigger than one of Harold Robbins'.'

'Well . . . I'm off then. You'll be all right, Arthur,' said Syrup.

'Thank you, Syrup.'

Chisholm brandished the note. 'You have an obligation as a citizen. It is your duty to help your local police –'

'He's asking you to grass,' said Terry helpfully.

'And why not?' snapped Chisholm, rounding on Terry. 'I

suppose that's a contemptuous word in your little vocabulary? What's wrong with giving a bit of information to us occasionally? I don't understand you people.'

'No, you don't,' said Terry. 'But just think it's a bit like the old school tie.'

'Yeah, that's why half of them would grass their granny,' Chisholm replied sarcastically.

'I have to agree with that, Mister Chisholm,' said Arthur sanctimoniously. 'It's the trend, innit? I blame the newspapers, see. If you can't rob a bank at least you can write an article about it in the *Sunday Times*. Not that I would know those sort of people.'

Then Terry said quietly, 'Syrup.'

'Eh?' asked Arthur, still very agitated.

Terry dashed to the door, hoping that he could grab Syrup but he was too late.

'What's all that about?' asked Chisholm menacingly.

'Search me, Mister Chisholm.'

'Yeah, I might. All kinds of things would leap to the eye.' He folded the twenty pound note and put it in his pocket.

'Are you gonna keep that?'

'Of course I am. You weren't going to use it?'

'Well, I thought I'd keep it as a souvenir.'

'And put it under the floorboards with the other souvenirs?' asked Chisholm sweetly.

'You should remember you're speaking to a respectable businessman,' said Arthur. There was sweat standing out on his forehead and he absentmindedly mopped at it with a silk handkerchief.

'Feeling warm, Arthur?' asked Chisholm.

'It's a little close in here, Mister Chisholm. I've told Dave he always keeps the place too hot.'

'I've got a place where we can cool you down, Arthur. It's called the nick.'

'Be reasonable, Mister Chisholm.'

'Yeah – I may be lenient this time, Arthur. But I'm watching you, right?'

'Yes, Mister Chisholm.'

'I'm watching your every move.'

The beautiful friendship between Arthur and Terry was over as the argument raged in the Jag, driven badly by a tense and impatient Arthur.

'And then you lose the Syrup!' Arthur was raging on. 'Gawd knows where he is now – the Mayfair Wig Centre? Or even Los Angeles. He's always fancied a syrup like Gene Kelly's.'

'He can't use the dough anyway,' said Terry defensively. 'Any idiot would recognise those hooky notes.'

Arthur treated him to a grim scowl. 'But I took 'em.'

'That's what I mean,' said Terry. 'You'd have to be a special kind of idiot.'

Arthur pumped the horn as he tried to overtake a car. 'I trusted that horrible Indian,' he moaned, ignoring Terry's insult.

'Yeah, you reckoned Shamy was a changed man.'

'That's because I've got compassion in my heart. Do-gooder? That's not my style. I'm going to "do" him – and do him good.' He glanced contemplatively at Terry, every bit the hard man. 'And I don't want any soft-hearted stuff from you. I want the old one-two. I want to see him splattered on the pavement, teeth in the gutter and plenty of claret an' all.'

Terry smiled sardonically, amused by Arthur's sudden blood-curdling threats. 'It could be that he's got a reasonable excuse.'

'How could he?' Arthur sounded completely outraged. 'He took a liberty.' He reflected for a while. 'No – not a liberty. We're talking about wickedness, a crime beyond human weakness – it's – it's *inhuman*.'

'It was only five hundred . . . wasn't it?'

'There you go,' said Arthur, 'a simple lad, you are. Trust – that's what we're talking about. I don't give 'em invoices, bills, receipts . . . I give 'em my hand and my heart.'

'I think they'd rather have a guarantee.'

'A mere slip of paper?' Arthur placed his hand on his heart. 'I give 'em my honour.'

'And you're about to ram this motor into a van,' warned Terry as Arthur steered wildly, his rage increasing all the while.

'You know what to do.'

Terry and Arthur were walking down the street towards the radio and video shop where they hoped to find the defaulting Shamy. Arthur had lost none of his fury.

'I'll have a chat with him,' said Terry mildly.

'I've told you what to do. The man needs a spanking.'

'Arthur –'

'Never mind, Arthur! He cheated me. He got me into bother with Chisholm – of all people. So he has to be taught a lesson. I don't want you to hang him, draw him, and quarter him. Just a reasonable retribution. Gawd help us – haven't you even seen Clint Eastwood?'

'Yeah – I'll throttle him with spaghetti.'

They arrived at the shop doorway and, strangely, Arthur's desire for confrontation appeared to subside as he hung back.

'Well, aren't you coming in?'

'Er . . . well, you'll be better on your own – I'm too generous hearted a man to witness such violence.'

Terry gave a dismissive snort and he went into the shop whilst Arthur, left to contemplate, lit up and watched Terry talking to Ajit. Then he glanced away and vaguely watched somebody crossing the road. Somebody familiar. It was Shamy, arguing with another Asian. In sudden panic Arthur fumbled with the door of the shop. 'Terry . . . Terry,' he yelped as Terry waved him away, still deep in conversation with Ajit. Failing to disturb him, Arthur bawled across the road.

'Oi – Shamy . . . Hey! You!'

Shamy turned, looked startled and said something quickly to his companion. Then he quickened his pace whilst Arthur turned back to the shop and began to pound desperately on the window. After what seemed like an eternity, Terry sensed Arthur's impatience.

'He's over there,' Arthur mouthed through the glass, with

an elaborate display of mime. When Terry came outside, Arthur said, 'Shamy –'

'Yeah – he's had the elbow,' said Terry.

'He's over there – you berk,' bellowed Arthur.

Terry glanced in the direction of Arthur's shaking finger and saw Shamy cutting down a side-street. Immediately, Terry ran across the road, with Arthur following him, yelling, 'Move it Terry – get your skates on.'

Shamy was running up the street and was about fifty yards in front of them.

'Don't let him get away,' shrieked Arthur, clutching at his hat and panting desperately.

'Shamy,' shouted Terry.

But Shamy wasn't going to stop. He glanced back as Terry sprinted behind him and then dashed into the front garden of a semi-detached cottage, scampering up the path to the small back garden. But Terry was closing in on him, encouraged by Arthur, now in the middle distance.

Shamy jumped over the low fence into the adjoining garden and over the next fence and the next and the next. After a few hundred yards of this massive bout of hurdling, Shamy was almost exhausted, panting, his heart pounding, his head aching. All the time he could hear Terry coming – and all the time his pace was slowing. Then Shamy stumbled and sprawled on his back, facing Terry with a beguiling smile.

'Hallo, Terry – I didn't realise it was you.' He finally managed to gasp out, effecting a look of pained surprise.

'Who did you think it was?'

'I know so many people –'

'And all of them running after you?'

Shamy gave a resigned smile. 'That's the story of my life, innit? How's Arthur?'

Arthur, meanwhile, was trying to track down the athletes by invading a number of different back gardens. In one of these he was discovered furtively lurking by an Indian housewife.

'Are you the man from the council?' she asked.

'Certainly not, madam.' He tipped his hat and beat a dignified retreat, leaving her staring after him in bewilderment.

Back in the street, Arthur saw Terry and Shamy. Slowly, menacingly, Arthur approached them.

'D'you want to hit him? Should I hold him?'

'What a deplorable suggestion.'

Terry looked surprised. 'I thought you wanted blood, Arthur.'

'We're civilised people. I'm sure there's a simple explanation . . . isn't there, Shamy?'

'Oh, yeah – course there is,' said Shamy relieved.

Arthur preserved an icy calm. 'I can't imagine what it is but nevertheless, I will listen to it.' He pointed to a pub down the road. 'Shall we imbibe?'

As Terry, Arthur and Shamy approached the pub, Shamy paused.

'There's just one thing.'

'Yeah?' asked Arthur suspiciously.

'There might be some people in there who I don't want to see.'

'Then have a little shufti – is that the word?'

Shamy agreed and opened the door, wondering why Arthur was being so helpful.

All the customers in the pub were Asian and the television was showing an Indian film. Once Shamy had had a good look round he said, 'OK.'

But Terry noticed he seemed surprised.

Arthur, Terry and Shamy sat down at a table.

'Terence,' said Arthur commandingly.

'Yeah?'

'Lay in some drinks.'

'Suppose he makes a dash for it?'

'I'll mind him.'

'You?'

'Besides,' Arthur smiled benignly at them both, 'I don't s'pose Shamy is in any mood for any more running.'

Reluctantly, Terry went to get the drinks. When he returned he found Arthur and Shamy sitting in deep silence.

'Chummy,' he said.

'I'm just waiting for a witness,' said Arthur grandly.

Shamy burst into agitated speech. 'See, I didn't know they was dodgy notes –'

Arthur gave him a patient smile. 'You're lying, Shamy.'

Shamy considered this for a moment and then he said, 'Yeah – you're right.'

'Did you make them yourself?'

'No, I bought them. A fiver for each note.'

'Oh, nice. You told me that the shop was yours too.'

'I never said that.'

Arthur's smile became definitely frosty. 'Oh yes you did.'

'Did I? Well, to be honest – I must've lied.'

Arthur stared at his glass and then glanced at Terry, who shrugged. 'See, you bought sewing machines from me and you sold them for – I assume – a handsome profit?'

'That's the point, Arthur – I owed money. Just ordinary debts, you know, a tenner here, a tenner there, plus cards, the gee-gees, gas bills, rates, the simple things. I worry about my wife, too. She works so hard and we needed a break so we had a couple of days in Eastbourne.' He paused. 'So I had to borrow some dough – then I needed some shoes.' Shamy appealed to Terry, 'You know what it's like –'

' 'Specially shoes.'

'Have you got *any* assets?' asked Arthur impatiently, returning the meeting to the agenda.

'Nothing.' He looked desperate. 'I'm one of nature's debtors, Arthur. I was in the red from birth.'

'Then you must've run up a few bills, eh?'

'To be honest, Arthur. You're at the end of a long line.'

'Aren't you ashamed?' asked Arthur sanctimoniously.

'I am – I am.' Shamy bowed his head.

'Well,' said Terry, 'as the man said . . . Annual income ten grand, annual expenditure nine and a half grand, well, I wouldn't call it happiness, but you can get by, can't you? Annual income ten grand, annual expenditure about twenty-five grand – and we're not only talking about misery, but a handful of aggravation.

'Nicely put, Terence,' said Arthur patronisingly.

'I'd drink to that,' said Shamy.

'If only you could call a round.' Arthur's voice was hollow.

'Might, in a few days.' He looked at them furtively. 'I've got a possibility –'

'Don't tell me,' said Arthur.

'I'm thinking of going into show business.'

'Yeah? Pantomime?'

Arthur frowned at Terry who was grinning and saying, 'Show business – Arthur's the expert in chick singers, if you're interested.'

'Ignore him,' said Arthur. 'He has a sense of humour.'

'Honest, Arthur,' said Shamy, 'I'm talking about the movie business.' His voice became a whisper. 'Video. Should I cut you in?'

'I'd love that . . . wouldn't I?' said Arthur sarcastically.

'They love a video.' He nudged Arthur and pointed towards the television screen. 'They make more films than Hollywood, you know.'

'All I want is my five hundred,' said Arthur resolvedly.

'Don't you trust me?'

Arthur stared at him – he just couldn't believe what he was saying. 'The simple answer,' began Arthur, but he was interrupted by a voice bellowing in his ear.

'You Shamy?'

'Oh, Christ –' Shamy half rose to his feet as a huge Sikh lunged across the table and almost knocked Arthur out of his chair.

'You owe me money,' said the Sikh.

'Don't you threaten me – I'm in the middle of a business meeting.' But Shamy looked far from confident.

'I don't give a damn about your white friends –'

'Tel?'

'They can't protect you –' He gestured to the other customers. 'These are all my countrymen.'

'And these are *my* countrymen,' said Shamy.

'Gawd help us,' sighed Arthur. 'Now he's gonna start a race riot.'

Shamy managed to talk his way out of his conflict with the Sikh – but only by promising to pay him in thirty-six hours. Grudgingly the Sikh had agreed – but Arthur and Terry knew he had about as much chance of getting his money back as Shamy buying him the Khyber Pass.

Now, Shamy, Arthur and Terry were standing in front of a shop window in Southall that displayed a vast mound of video tapes – all of Indian films.

'Look at that one,' said Shamy. 'It's like *Gone With The Wind* with a dash of *Dallas* and *Death Wish*. Biggest thing since – I don't know. If you've got a film like that, it's a licence to print money.'

'You know all about it.'

'I was just trying to get some easy money. But as you said, nobody gets money without working.'

'*He* said that?'

'Yeah, I think.'

'It is the cornerstone of my philosophy –' said Arthur pompously.

'Look,' Terry's voice was incredulous, 'you took some sewing machines from one place to another place, that's not exactly philosophy.'

'You have to think about it,' said Arthur.

'I agree with you, Arthur.' Shamy was quick to curry favour.

'What?' asked Terry outraged.

'What *he* said. You've gotta work, you have to seize the opportunities. Like I've got –' He began to whisper urgently. 'I've got this tape – the biggest Indian film ever.'

'*E.T.*, *Gandhi*, you name it –'

'Then you're gonna be rich.' Arthur walked on, he simply didn't want to know about any more of Shamy's schemes.

'But I need help. I need –'

'I know what you're going to say . . . You're gonna say you need money?'

'Well, sort of –'

'Goodbye.' Arthur walked briskly away with Shamy tugging on his sleeve. 'Terence,' said Arthur, 'this man is molesting me.'

'This is the best offer you've had today.'

'He is importuning me –'

'A few measly pounds –'

'There's a by-law against this.'

'Arthur!'

Arthur walked to his car and Shamy looked at Terry. 'You understand, don't you?' he said desperately.

'Well, just for once,' Terry said in a considered voice, 'he may be right.'

'Why can't people trust me?' asked Shamy naively, looking at Terry, hoping he would confirm his honesty.

'You've got a reputation and it ain't for honesty.'

'All right – all right. Occasionally, I tell fibs –'

'No . . . you're a liar.'

Shamy considered that for a moment. 'Yeah. All right. But I'm in an 'ole. I know that – but how can I get out?'

Across the road, Arthur got into his Jag and shouted to Terry. 'Let's go.'

'Listen – just give me half-an-hour of your time tomorrow – thirty minutes, that's all. A jam-jar from A to B – is that a terrible request? We're friends . . . not friends – *mates*! Would you do that for me? I've got to collect this tape – I'm skint, I haven't even got the fare for a cab. Tomorrow, eh?'

To avoid any more pleading, Terry agreed.

'You're one of the good guys, Terry.'

'Don't I know it – an' all.'

An impatient Arthur was revving up, when Terry opened the passenger door. Shamy then came up to Arthur and stood optimistically by the bonnet of the Jag.

'Any chance of a lift home, Arthur?'

There was a long moment before Arthur delivered his considered and crushing reply.

'Piss off.' Then he gunned the engine and Shamy stepped away.

'Cheers, Arthur. I was gonna walk anyway.'

The Jaguar disappeared down the road and Shamy began slowly to walk home. But he had not gone far when an elderly Indian shouted at him from across the road, 'Shamy, I want to see you –'

Shamy gave him a tentative wave. 'I've got to dash,' he said and began, somewhat wearily, to run. His legs felt very stiff, but Shamy knew that he had to keep running.

'It's important,' yelled the Indian.

'Yeah, I know. See you.'

'Bloody man. Where is my money?' He began to limp after the rapidly disappearing Shamy. But gradually the gap widened.

Arthur was muttering fiercely to himself as he drove the Jag through the dense traffic.

'What did you say?' asked Terry.

'I said, I'm getting soft.'

'Well, when were you hard?'

'In my prime. Before I met you. Nobody took liberties in those days. That little Indian would've been odds on for a kneecap job.'

'Leave it out, Arthur.' Terry was adamant. 'You'd faint if you saw a bare kneecap, never mind the blood.'

A few miles away, Chisholm was parking his Sierra outside the Wigwam Hair Centre, a down-market wig shop. Chisholm glanced at the models in the window and his companion, D.C. Jones, said, 'I don't think they're my style.'

Without deigning to comment, Chisholm marched into the Hair Centre where he stood for a while examining the wad of twenty pound notes whilst the owner watched him. He was a large burly man with hairy arms, an open-neck shirt, displaying a hairy chest, and a handsome head of hair.

'Can I help you?' he asked.

'I don't see why not,' said Chisholm, showing his identity and explaining his business.

The owner, whose name was Mr Henry, went to check the

till. When he returned, he said, 'Fifteen of them. Three hundred.'

'Didn't you check them?'

'You don't, do you. You wouldn't think a man with a scalp problem would do that.'

'Could you describe him?'

'Well, he's wearing, at this moment, one of our Roger Moore's. Very popular, completely waterproof.'

'Waterproof?'

'Keep the rain off.'

'Off what? Their brains?'

'You can swim with a Roger Moore. We have our exclusive, special adhesive –'

'Well, apart from glue on his scalp, are there any other distinctive features?'

'I'd call him nondescript – more-or-less.'

'No scars, moles, a big hooter and dodgy eye?' asked Chisholm disappointedly.

'As I say – nondescript, average . . . a face in a crowd. Mind you, I'd recognise his scalp anywhere.'

Chisholm gave a manic smile of angry frustration. 'We don't have a file of cranium prints.'

'There is one thing – what you might call a clue. He left his other wig.' He rummaged in a drawer, coming out with the soiled, battered Engelbert Humperdink creation. 'A cheap nylon hairpiece,' said Mr Henry fastidiously. 'Circa 1972, an early, I would say – Engelbert Humperdink. I'm afraid it needs renovation.'

Chisholm carefully picked up the greasy looking wig. 'Renovation? It's got real dandruff.' His lips were parted in disgust.

'Not in the best of condition.'

'I've seen nicer rats down the old East Indian Dock, Jonesie – try this on.'

'Me? What have I done?' said Jones indignantly.

'D'you want a list? We are trying to picture the face beneath this – this apparition. Try it.'

Mr Henry helped Jones to fit the wig on his cranium.

Eventually, Jones looked in a mirror and started back. 'I feel like a real fool.'

'True . . . true.' Then he reacted. 'The Syrup!'

'What? Who?'

'A person known to the police.' He turned to Mr Henry. 'I will have to take this Irish into custody. Have you got a plastic bag or something?'

'Course. You mean, you know the culprit?'

'Oh, yes. I suppose you could say that he's got a price on his head –' Chisholm smirked whilst Jones hooted with polite laughter.

Mr Henry took the wig off Jones and put it into a plastic bag. 'It's an incredible piece of deduction, Sergeant. Incidentally, have you ever thought of having a hairpiece yourself?'

'Why?' Chisholm gave him a sour glance as Mr Henry looked at his head.

'Well, I hope you don't mind my saying so, but you are receding a bit, sir, almost to the point of vanishing.'

'I get by,' said Chisholm, a strained look on his face.

'I'm sure, but it is a disability. Socially, even professionally. I'm sure that your macho image would be enhanced with, say, the Burt Reynolds model that we offer. Or even the Starsky, which is very popular with the upper ranks at the Yard.'

'I was going to suggest that to you, guv,' said Jones happily.

'Were you?'

'Yes, I was. But –' Jones's voice trailed away as he recognised that certain strange gleam in Chisholm's eyes. Jones spoke quickly. 'Only joking, guv. Should I carry the plastic bag?'

Shamy arrived home at his flat a shaken man.

'Gayle?'

'In the kitchen. You want tea?' yelled a girl's voice.

'Please.' He took off his jacket and saw a handbag on a chair. 'Anything happened?'

'Just a sec.'

Taking advantage of his girl-friend's absence, Shamy quickly opened the handbag and took out a purse. He grabbed a few pounds, closed the handbag, went over to a dresser and opened a drawer. Inside there was a wad of twenty pound notes. He counted them and then stuffed them into his pocket. 'Have you taken some twenty pound notes from that drawer?'

'Yeah.' The mystery voice entered the room, carrying two cups of tea, revealing herself as an attractive blonde in her late twenties. 'I took forty pounds to pay the gas bill; they were going to cut us off.' Gayle gave Shamy the cup of tea and kissed him on the cheek.

'And they took 'em?'

'Why not?'

'Well, you know –'

'What, exactly?'

'You shouldn't have used them.'

'Oh my God!' Gayle suddenly realised what she had done. 'Are they duds?'

Shamy sat down and nodded. 'There are hundreds of them around.'

'They even gave me change.'

Shamy grinned. 'Then we've got a result, haven't we?'

'Haven't you got any shame?'

'Don't start all that again – I'm having a run of bad luck.'

Gayle slumped miserably onto the sofa. 'There's even more. Some other bloke was trying to get hold of you . . . Kamal, or somebody.'

'I only borrowed £50 from him.'

'Well he wants it, and he's bringing his brother tomorrow.'

'I tell you what – I'll never borrow from him again.'

'I don't somehow think he'll let you.' Gayle looked at Shamy with an expression of pity mixed with amusement. She knew him so well. 'I dunno, why can't you work like all other Indians?'

'You'd like that – wouldn't you?'

'Yeah. You don't even like curry! *Everybody* likes curry.'

'Some English people don't like it; and I'm one of them. You've got all these romantic views of the East, the Taj Mahal –'

'You thought it was a caff in the Commercial Road.'

'And you see too much television. Come on, be nice to me, eh?' He leant across to her, hoping that she would be less abrasive. She hesitated and then hugged him.

'What am I going to do with you?' she asked, this time torn between love and desperation.

'I've had a hard day, y'know.'

Chisholm was sitting in a steamy café at a dirty table, to which Jones had just brought two slopped cups of tea. He stirred his tea and stared at the street as he soliloquised.

'Did I let him off the hook? He actually had a dud twenty pound note in his hand. Bang to rights. And I let him get away. There should be no pity for the likes of Daley and his ilk.'

Jones said nothing, knowing that Chisholm wished to speak aloud and uninterrupted.

'The Syrup was talking to him. Then, a few hours later the same person turned over a wig-maker and scarpered with a Roger Moore look-alike toupee. Is that mere fortuitousness? I think not.'

'I agree, guv,' said Jones, thinking it was time to at least prove his existence.

But Chisholm didn't even hear him. 'Of course, there are more important things in life than nicking Daley. But at this moment I can't think of anything else. Daley – he's a thorn in my flesh, a tickle in my throat. I had hair when I started in this manor. I've had many encounters with Daley and most of them are nasty. I don't approve of his pathetic, trivial wheezes – gold-fish, Albanian sparkling wine or even flood-damaged bathing suits –'

'You have to laugh, though.'

For the first time Chisholm heard him. 'No,' he said.

'He got that micro-oven for our canteen.'

'Burnt offerings. I've always thought of Daley as a more

dangerous man. The idea of him circulating dodgy twenty pound notes is attractive – for the likes of us. Even better if he's actually *printing* currency of the realm.'

'That's a staggering thought.'

'Awesome,' said Chisholm with a kind of secret delight.

Terry honked the horn of his battered car and Shamy ran out of his flat and got in.

'Where are we going?' asked Terry, already cursing himself for weakening.

'Down the shops. I'll only be there for a couple of minutes. I've got to meet a guy –'

'What about?' asked Terry bleakly.

'A dog,' said Shamy.

A supervisor was checking an Indian film in a video factory. Around them were banks of cassettes and a familiar figure – Mr Mitra. Holding a cassette, Mr Mitra walked to the main entrance, on to the street and into his family saloon car.

Fifty yards down the road was another car – an old Cortina – and as Mr Mitra's saloon passed the intersection, the Cortina began to follow him. Unknown to him, the two occupants were plain-clothed police officers.

'I'll only be a couple of minutes,' said Shamy as he got out of Terry's car outside the video shop.

'Make it snappy,' warned the suspicious Terry. 'I'm not hanging around, you know.'

As Shamy stood outside the shop, he saw Mr Mitra's saloon pulling in. As he parked and opened the door, Shamy saw that Mr Mitra had the video cassette in his hand. Quickly he walked towards him and, in a sudden movement, grabbed the video cassette and shoved Mr Mitra into the shopway. Then he ran off towards the side street where Terry's car was parked.

At the same time, the Cortina skidded to a halt and the two plain-clothed police officers dashed to Mr Mitra.

'You're nicked, mister,' said one of them as he grabbed him.

'I've been attacked,' Mitra protested.

Shamy sat panting in the front seat of Terry's car. 'Let's go,' he said, gasping but Terry had no idea of what was going on.

'What's up?' he asked, his suspicion deepening.

'Nothing. I've just got to see somebody.' He gave Terry a quick, nervous smile.

Terry started the car and began to drive at normal speed. Shamy glanced through the rear window agitatedly.

'I've got away with it. Hey, how about that?'

'You nicked that video, didn't you?'

'Course not.'

'Then how come you're so excited?'

'No, I'm not.'

'Yeah?'

'Straight.'

Terry shrugged. 'You know what, my old son?'

'Yeah?'

'I don't believe a bleedin' word you're saying.'

Meanwhile, outside the video shop, the two plain-clothed police officers were frisking Mr Mitra.

'Don't you understand, I was mugged,' Mitra protested.

'He hasn't got it,' said one of the police officers to the other, in a disgruntled voice.

'Daylight robbery –' continued Mitra.

'Shurrup – you're a lucky man.'

'Can't we nick him anyway?'

The other police officer frowned. 'Not today,' he said.

'Who're you expecting to follow us?' asked Terry as Shamy kept looking through the rear window.

'Nobody.'

'Then why're you looking through the back window?'

'No, I wasn't.'

Terry gave him a very dubious glance. 'Where are we actually going?'

'What about your place?'

'No.' He was quite decisive. Then he said, 'You did nick it, didn't you?'

'Honestly,' began Shamy. Then he said, 'Yeah, I did. He nicked it anyway –'

'That's all right, is it?'

'Sort of. The only thing is, they know about it.'

'Didn't you think about that beforehand?' said Terry fatalistically.

'You don't, do you?'

'I dunno – you tell me.'

'Balaclavas and false beards – I can't be doing with them.'

'Now they're after you?'

'Yeah.' He gave a smile of resignation and even Terry had to laugh.

'What about Arthur? Could I stay at his place?'

'You must be kidding. You couldn't kip on his floor even if you paid his £500 plus 100 per cent interest.'

'He's so suspicious, isn't he? But I know a place,' said Shamy. 'It's not far from where you live.'

'Oh my Gawd,' said Terry. 'Can't we make it Birmingham?'

Terry and Shamy stood before the scruffy Paddington hotel reception desk.

'Both of you?' asked the middle-aged manager quizzically.

Shamy gave him a charming smile. 'We're not *all* that friendly. It's just me.'

'Got any luggage?'

'It's at the station,' said Terry.

'Thirty pounds a night. In advance.'

'Okay.' Shamy pulled out his wad of twenties and gave him two notes and the Manager lugubriously gave him a ten pound note as change.

'Room service?' asked Shamy hopefully.

'Continental breakfast – two pounds extra. You can have a curry across the road.'

Shamy gave him a bleak smile. 'Thanks.'

In the middle of the forecourt of Arthur's used car lot stood a Fiesta on which a scruffy looking character called Smudger was fixing a roof sign. It read:

DaLey
Driving School
Qualified Instructors Approved

Arthur beamed at him in an avuncular manner.

'It looks like a real driving school,' said Smudger happily.

'Well it is.'

'No disrespect, Arthur – but what's all that about, "approved"?'

'They all have that.'

'Yeah, but approved by who?'

'Me.'

Smudger grinned. 'Yeah, I've got it. This is gonna be a winner. Incidentally, have you got a licence for me? Just in case –'

'In case of what?'

'If I get a pull.'

'You're supposed to be a driving instructor,' said Arthur severely.

'That was years ago. I *had* a licence, but I lost it.'

'Well – apply for another.'

'It was in a different name, wannit?'

'You come in here as a bona fide instructor –'

'I never said that. I taught my brother.'

'He's in Ford Open Prison.'

'But *not* for a driving offence.'

'What for then?' asked Arthur gloomily.

'Stolen motor – but nothing wrong with his driving. Sweet as a nut.'

Arthur was about to make some condemning remark when the telephone began to ring. Arthur walked sullenly over to his caravan. 'You've misled me,' he said sadly.

But Smudger was unrepentant. 'You must've been Brahms that night.'

Once in the office, Arthur picked up the phone. 'The Daley School of Motoring,' he said in a posh voice.

'You what?' said Terry.

'It's a new venture, Terence,' said Arthur grandly. 'Can I help you?'

'You know what we were talking about – films?'

'If it's Shamy – the answer is –'

'All right, all right. But he wants to see you and we're not talking about phony notes.'

'Look, every time I see him it costs me money.'

'This time it won't,' said Terry.

'I'll see him,' returned Arthur. 'One little thing, has he got a driving licence?'

Downstairs at reception, the manager put down the phone and thought for a while. Then he went to the till and took out several twenty pound notes. He picked up the first two notes and examined them. Then he picked up the telephone and dialled.

Arthur, watched attentively by the manager, arrived at the hotel room half-an-hour later and immediately plunged into an argument with Shamy. At the same time, Terry was trying to convince Arthur to at least bend an unprejudiced ear.

'How much?'

'About three hundred and fifty.'

'Did you hear that? This man who owes me –'

'It seems a good deal to me,' said Terry calmly.

Arthur turned on him sarcastically. 'Have you gotta healthy bank balance? How's your investments? And the old portfolio – is that thriving? What are you into these days? Commodities, unit trusts, bricks and mortar?'

'Then don't ask me,' shrugged Terry.

'I won't,' said Arthur firmly.

'But I've got an idea that you don't understand what he's saying.'

'I understand it perfectly. He wants to go to Bombay and buy a video tape there.'

'That's not it! I'm selling – not buying.'

'That's what I said.'

'No, you didn't.'

Before Arthur started again, Shamy said, 'They can't get video tapes in India. See. This film is the biggest thing since sliced bread or instant rice. They copy them over here for the western market and Africa, for example. We're not worried about the shops in Southall, or Leeds or Bradford – we're selling to millions. Every village in India has got its own video. If I take six copies to Bombay, to a certain person, then we'll be rich. One hundred grand and for *me*, that's rich.'

Arthur stared at him, a certain comprehension dawning.

'I knew you didn't understand it,' said Terry looking blank.

'All I need is a return ticket to Bombay and a couple of pounds for food and hotel and Bob's your uncle.'

'It can't be that easy?'

'But it is,' said Shamy. 'It really is.'

If only Arthur had realised that Chisholm was downstairs examining twenty pound notes, he would not have been so interested.

'Indian – you reckon?' asked Chisholm of the Manager.

'Of that persuasion I would say.'

Chisholm turned to his constant companion, Jones. 'I think we're in luck. Would you like to lead the way?' he asked the manager delightedly.

'There's one little problem,' said Arthur. 'If you go to Bombay we may never see you again –'

'I don't even like the food. Are you going to help me or not?'

Then there came the gentlest of knocks on the door.

'Room service?' asked Arthur.

The manager stood back as Chisholm and Jones stepped over

the threshold and an expression of euphoria crossed Chisholm's face as he saw Arthur. 'It must be my birthday.'

'What a pleasant surprise, Mr Chisholm.'

'I bet it is. You can introduce me to your friend with the fistful of twenty pound notes.'

'Gawd help us,' said Arthur.

Shamy didn't wait for the introductions. He pushed Terry aside, bowled over Chisholm and dashed down the corridor like a whippet. Jones and Chisholm charged after him. The manager followed.

Arthur and Terry were alone in the hotel room. Terry picked up the video tape and put it in his pocket. 'What d'you reckon?'

Arthur gave an expressive shrug. 'I think Mr Chisholm's gone to take some exercise. I wonder if he's any good at hurdling?'

But Terry was not to be free of Shamy for long. That night he was woken by a tapping on the window. Terry dragged himself out of bed, went to the window and opened the curtain. It was, of course, Shamy. Terry went to the door and switched on the light. Shamy stumbled in, looking terrible.

'You been running all night?'

'Bloody freezing.'

'What time is it?' He asked as he closed the door.

'Five o'clock.'

'Great. You're taking a chance coming here, aren't you?'

'And you –'

'I haven't done anything.'

'You haven't got a fire?'

Terry switched on a double-bar electric fire as Shamy rubbed miserably at his arms.

'That copper was after the twenty pound notes, not the video.'

'That's enough, innit?' Terry went into the kitchen to make a cup of tea. 'Why didn't you go home?'

'Because the Indians are after me. I didn't know where to

go, so I walked the streets. This city's dead at three o'clock in the morning. Just four taxis and the odd patrol car. And you feel *guilty* . . . I thought, I'd mingle with the crowds at Paddington Station. Ever tried that?'

'Not really.'

'There's no trains. Half a dozen penny stamps and two old Bill walking around the place, you feel very conspicuous, y'know.' He warmed his hands. 'Is Arthur still on about me going to Bombay?'

'I think so.'

Shamy took out his wad of twenty pound notes and looked at them. 'I want to get rid of these.' He held them to the electric fire and Terry kicked a waste-paper bin towards him.

'Just before you burn up the house –'

Shamy stared down at the flames. 'Pity, I thought they were good.'

'Ever thought of getting a job?'

'Eh?'

'They usually say that to me. But you, you're in a different class.'

'I don't believe in it. If God wanted us to clock in every day he would've given us a time-card in our hands.'

'Yeah, but you have to work *hard* to avoid work.'

'Well, what d'you want me to be? Somebody like Arthur? I agree, he's a grafter – but is he happy?'

'When he has a roll-call every night, he's delighted.'

'But happy? I don't know. Happiness is the thing you do after work.'

The next day an attractive young woman called Denise was waiting beside the Daley School of Motoring car. Looking both aggressive and impatient, she kept glancing towards the caravan where Arthur was talking on the phone.

'She's here, Smudger,' he was saying. 'Your first pupil. Well, how long is that going to take? As quick as you can then.' He hung up and went outside, rubbing his hands together ingratiatingly. 'Alas, one of my instructors has been detained, but he'll be along in about half-an-hour.'

'Well, can't you take me?'

'*I* am the principal,' he said with dignity.

'You can drive, can't you?'

'Young lady. . . I, personally, have taught the highest and the lowest, advanced motorists and those who don't know the difference between a slip-differential and a windscreen wiper –'

'Well, you'll do then, or I'll have to push off.'

'Have you actually put down a deposit yet?'

'No.'

'Well, in that case – could I suggest a preliminary course of, say six lessons – at our introductory offer of sixty sovs.'

'Fair enough.' She brought out a wad of twenty pound notes and gave three to Arthur.

'Thank you, darling,' said Arthur and immediately checked the notes against the light.

'What's all that about?'

'You can't be too careful.'

'Well, give 'em back then. What am I – the phantom forger?' She tried to retrieve the money, which was difficult with Arthur clutching three of the notes.

'Did I suggest that?' asked Arthur calmingly. 'Never in a million years did I say that, luv. But there's hundreds of Sexton Blakes all over the place. Haven't you read about it in the local rag?'

'Well, I don't mix with those sorts of people.'

'Of course you don't. But there's some terrible scallywags in the world.' He took the notes and put them in his pocket. 'I'll start you off on the right foot by giving you a preliminary lesson. At least pro temp, as it were, till Smudger appears.'

Denise went to the car whilst Arthur followed, having another quick peak at the notes.

'I know the rudiments. I mean, I've failed the test four times. Of course, they're against me.'

'Who?'

'All of *them*. They don't like my attitude.' She got into the car and slammed the door, whilst Arthur slid warily into the passenger seat. Just as Denise was about to switch on the engine, he said:

'Now, now, young lady. Let's do it right. Check your door, seat belt and so on.'

'Yeah, yeah, yeah.'

Arthur was both pedantic and avuncular. 'I trust you have mastered the four principles of the internal combustion engine?'

'Eh?'

'Induction, compression, ignition –'

'And then bloody exhaustion.'

Arthur looked surprised. 'Very good. You obviously know quite a lot. I think we should go into the street and see what –'

Denise quickly switched on the engine, but Arthur was still not ready. 'Just a minute. I haven't finished yet. Right away, I see that you've missed a crucial point. Young lady, your mirror is your friend.'

'We're in a yard.'

'Doesn't matter. It should be automatic. Where're you going?' The car was creeping towards the road.

'I don't know –'

'Brake, brake –'

'Well, haven't you got one?'

Arthur pointed vaguely to the floor. 'The middle one . . . your foot –' He grabbed the hand-brake. '– Take off the other pedal –'

'Which one?'

'The one your foot's on.'

The car stopped dead.

'I don't know why you're so excited.'

'I'm not excited,' said Arthur practically gibbering. 'But you must understand it's quite difficult to stop the motor if you've got your foot on the accelerator.'

'Well, the other cars had pedals for the teachers as well.'

'Yeah, but that way you won't learn so much. My system – the Daley-way, every day's another day – you learn from your own mistakes. Like Fittabaldie and all the others.'

Denise ignored him. 'Can we go somewhere? I ain't gonna sit in a yard all day.'

'All in good time, my dear.'

'We could shoot down to Sussex to see my old dad. He knows you, anyway.'

'Who?'

'Big Alfie –'

'Alfie the Hammer?'

'Yeah and when I told him that I was having lessons from you he said – you should be with him in Ford Open Prison. Where're we going then?'

Arthur was a little taken aback. 'I think first I'll sus out your ability . . . gears, clutch, your road sense –'

'I know all that.'

'I'm sure . . . It's Denise, innit . . . But I'd like to see it for meself. Let's go down the street and then –' He looked alarmed as she gunned the engine. 'Not yet –' He grew a fraction calmer.

'All right.'

Arthur quickly fastened his seat belt, testing it, checking it and checking it again. 'Right . . . a nice bit of clutchwork, an easy gear-change and we're gonna go left . . . LEFT.' His voice ended on a high note and there was a sickening crunch as Denise engaged first gear. The car lurched ahead and steered to the right. Without heed to the passing traffic, Denise drove confidently out of the yard and there was a terrible sound of skidding as another car narrowly avoided them.

'I said, "left",' said Arthur weakly.

'What does it matter?' asked Denise happily.

Arthur looked dazed, as if he was on the verge of a nervous breakdown. 'I think it does. If I say "left" and then you turn – Oh my gawd . . . brake, brake –'

For a horrendous moment, it looked as if Denise was about to smash into a car in front. But, astonishingly, Denise not only avoided the car, but also overtook it.

'Very good,' said Arthur weakly, glancing into the rear window. 'Look at his boat – ashen, that's the word – ashen. You see, Denise, you might think it doesn't matter if I say "left" and you go right. Of course in the cosmic way it's not all that important, but for mere mortals, like meself, it becomes confusing. Do you understand?'

'Yeah.'

'There *is* a difference between left and right –'

Denise spoke abruptly. 'All right – sod it then – we'll go the other way.' She suddenly span the steering-wheel and executed a hair-raising U-turn.

A number of expressions passed across Arthur's face but the most recognisable were fear, agony, shock and mad, mad hope that soon this nightmare might come to an end.

Smudger was sitting on the caravan steps when the car, driven by Denise, shuddered to a halt on the forecourt. He got up and opened the passenger door. Inside Arthur was staring ahead.

'You all right, Arthur?'

'Yeah – good as gold,' he said, his voice distant and his eyes still fixed. Beside him, Denise yawned. She looked totally relaxed.

'You look a bit queer.'

'No, no.'

'I got the licence, see.'

'Nice.' Arthur unfastened the seat belt and got out of the car. He walked slowly towards the caravan with Smudger beside him.

'I mean, it's a good 'un,' Smudger whispered. 'Not in my name, obviously, but similar.'

'That's nice,' said Arthur again. He fumbled for his keys.

'Did you have a good lesson?' asked Smudger innocently.

Arthur stared at him for a moment. Then he closed his eyes. 'Smudger, it was awful. Never mind her dad, she ought to be locked up.' He decided not to unlock the door and instead went to his Jaguar. 'I'm going to my warehouse. I don't want to be here when you come back.'

'Right, Arthur,' said Smudger as he turned back to Denise and her demon driving.

When Arthur was about to open up his lock-up, he paused, detecting a presence. Mr Mitra was about two inches from his face.

Arthur smiled. 'Dear oh dear, you did give me a nasty turn.'

But Mr Mitra didn't answer. When Arthur looked closely he saw there was another Indian behind him – and another, and another. When he spun round he saw two more. For a moment, Arthur thought he was having a nightmare. Then reality intruded – there was something menacing about the Indians.

He smiled hopefully. 'Buying or selling, gentlemen?'

'Please open the door and enter,' said Mr Mitra.

'I was gonna do that anyway. Can I help you?'

'Absolutely. Lead on,' he said. Somewhat reluctantly, Arthur opened the door and the Indians filed in.

'Brothers?' asked Arthur.

'Brothers in arms,' replied Mr Mitra, closing the door.

Arthur sighed, feeling the world crowding in on him again.

'I understand that you have an article of mine.'

' I do business with lots of Indians –'

'My video tape?'

'That's what it's all about. I'm afraid you've got the wrong man. I deal in many things –'

'Shamy stole my video. I want it back. Please sit down.' He pointed to a chair and Arthur realised that he must comply. He sat down heavily. 'There is no nonsense about this,' Mr Mitra explained carefully. 'We are going to search this place piece by piece, brick by brick and – eventually – bone by bone.' He turned to his colleagues. 'Begin,' he said commandingly.

'I haven't got it,' said Arthur.

'They're very careful. Would you like a cigar?' He sat down

and offered Arthur an expensive cigar. Arthur began to cheer up.

'A man of discernment, I see.'

'Among other things. I'm also a wholesale tobacconist.'

'This could be your lucky day. Interested in some good cigarillos? Argentinian, as it happens. But with the political backlash, it's quite difficult to move 'em.'

'No, thank you.'

'Well, there's all kinds of things here –'

'I have three corner shops, four newsagents and a couple of Do-It-Yourself shops.'

'Paint? Five litre pots.' Arthur was ever pressing. 'Perfect for the handyman. These are very similar to the paint used by the council – what we call Institutional Green –'

'Stolen goods,' said Mr Mitra censoriously.

'Surplus stock,' replied Arthur indignantly.

Then one of the Indians called to Mr Mitra and said something in Urdu. He was carrying some boxes. 'Stack them up outside,' commanded Mr Mitra.

As the Indian went outside, Arthur said, 'Careful with them. Have they done this before?' he asked Mr Mitra.

Chisholm emerged from the Magistrates Court and walked to his car, carrying a piece of paper in his hand. Once inside, and with Jones driving, he gave an icy smile of satisfaction. 'They don't like it, y'know. A search warrant is like winning the pools in our game.'

'I never trust magistrates anyway, guv.'

'They're always worried about rights.'

'Whose rights, eh?'

'I can't wait to see Daley's boat. He'll be on the old trombone in two seconds.'

'To whom?'

'The whole team – the busy-bodies. Release, Split, The Samaritans, Mensa, Exist, The London Rape Centre, The Alternative Parents' Group, Gay Rights – the whole shmeer, including the Royal bleeding Automobile Club.' Chisholm looked lovingly at the warrant.

After a pause, Jones said, 'Going to the Federation meeting on Monday?'

Chisholm scowled at him. 'What have they ever done for me?'

A pile of boxes began to grow outside the door of the lock-up, whilst inside seven of the Indians were making a systematic search. Then, one of them uncovered a video machine and some cassettes beneath a pile of leg-warmers. 'Mr Mitra –' He showed him one of the video cassettes.

'Is this mine?'

'No, no, it's an old one.'

'What does it say?'

'*Gone With The Wind*,' said one of the Indians.

'Like so many other things in this gaff,' said Arthur sadly.

Mr Mitra crossed the room and took the tape. He picked up another cassette. '*To Catch A Thief*,' he read.

'One of the greats. Can I mark your card?'

Mr Mitra picked up another tape. 'You mean, this one?'

'No, no – that's not the title,' said Arthur hastily. 'What I'm saying is that these videos are from another era. I'm not interested in your sort of films.'

'Really? Well, Mr Daley, I am going to mark *your* card. Do you know about Ghandi?'

'One of your own.'

'He believed in passive resistance.'

'A noble sentiment. We need a bit of that these days, eh?'

'Not me. Kill the bastards,' he said.

'Fair's fair – that's a bit strong, innit?'

Mr Mitra put his arm round Arthur's shoulders. 'There are some Indians who believe in turning the other cheek and the meek will inherit the world. Silly sods. There is another tradition, Arthur – you don't mind me calling you Arthur?'

'An honour.'

'Warriors, for example. Juggernauts, the thuggee, and those chaps could certainly have a good row. In my youth I saw howling mobs, baying for the blood of young Tommy

Atkins. Not a pleasant sight, Arthur.' As Mr Mitra spoke, the other Indians gathered silently around Arthur. 'Have you got my drift, Arthur,' continued Mr Mitra. 'In other words – if I may use an apt expression – you're up the Khyber. You've got ten seconds.'

Arthur looked uneasily around the circle. Four seconds had gone before Arthur plucked up the courage to say, 'You've got it all wrong –'

'Six,' said Mr Mitra.

A loud knock interrupted their deliberation and at the same time the door burst open. Chisholm stood there, looking at Arthur.

'What's this then? A Dutch auction – or even a Doolali auction?'

'How nice to see you, Mister Chisholm.' He turned courteously to Mr Mitra. 'D'you know Detective Sergeant Chisholm, a leading local representative of the thin blue line?'

Mr Mitra gave Chisholm a pleasant smile. 'Well, I suppose you have lots of business to do. Good morning, Mister Daley, and to you, Sergeant.' Mr Mitra beckoned to his troops and in single-file they marched out. Each of them acknowledging Chisholm as they took their leave, muttering "Good morning". Chisholm looked at them suspiciously.

'See you again, lads,' said Arthur cheerily.

Chisholm stared at Arthur as the last Indian closed the door behind him. 'What are you selling now? Second-hand poppadums?'

'I also like to do my bit for race relations, Mr Chisholm.'

Chisholm ignored him and began to prowl around the lock-up.

'Can I help you?' asked Arthur, after a while.

But Chisholm only scowled at him, still silently pacing. Jones picked up a couple of transistor radios on a shelf and Chisholm looked at Arthur's desk. He opened a drawer, rummaging through the contents and was eventually interrupted in his task by Arthur.

'D'you mind? These are personal effects.'

Chisholm pulled the drawer out and tipped the contents on to the desk-top.

'It's a bit presumptious. I do have certain rights, you know.'

'Like what?'

'You're trespassing on private property. Unless you've got a magistrates' search warrant, sworn and signed and sealed –'

With tremendous satisfaction, Chisholm produced the warrant. 'All right? D'you wanna call the Law Centre, Citizens Advice Bureau, or Channel Four? I think not. The best thing you should do is sit down or, even better – get down on your knees and pray that we don't find anything.'

Arthur looked shocked. 'Mister Chisholm – what have I done?'

'All kinds of things. I was hoping to see a printing press –'

'Why?'

'Somebody's printing these twenty pound notes.'

Greatly relieved, Arthur sat down. He smiled. 'Would I do that?'

'Yes,' replied Chisholm curtly. He was rummaging through another drawer.

'After all these years. You *know me* –'

'Yes.' Chisholm's voice was still hard. He unfurled a roll of labels that he had taken from the drawer. 'Miss Selfridges? See – you'd do anything for a penny or a pound. And for a twenty pound note, you'd mortgage your soul.'

'That's a very offensive remark, Mister Chisholm.'

'I've been saving that up.' He started to pace around again. 'Why have I come to see you? Forged notes have been wafting around the manor – I first saw one in your own hand. At this moment a man is impersonating Roger Moore; he doesn't *really* look like him, but the hair is similar. This person is known as The Syrup, an acquaintance of yours, and he bought the Roger Moore toupee with fifteen dud twenty pound notes. Last night I attempted to apprehend an Indian who was trying to pass – guess what – twenty pound notes. What is the common denominator? All roads lead to Daley –'

Arthur looked relaxed and confident. 'Search, then, Mr Chisholm.'

Chisholm looked at him and there was doubt in his eyes. Could Arthur have escaped him again? Chisholm turned abruptly to Jones. 'Have you found anything?'

'All kinds of remarkable things, guv – everlasting pencils –'

'Just a gimmick,' said Arthur airily.

'Scotch . . . *Loch* Eim?'

'Jews say that.'

'Yeah, well, it's for the discerning Jewish Scotch drinker. I cater for many palates.'

'And most of them reprobates.'

The telephone rang and Arthur and Chisholm reached for it at the same time. Arthur won by a narrow margin. 'Daley Enterprises.' At the same time, Chisholm put the receiver to his ear. It was Terry.

'It's me. I'm with Shamy. He wants some dough to get his ticket, there's a flight this afternoon. We'll shoot over, eh?'

Arthur had little to say.

'Who's with you?' asked Terry, getting wind of trouble.

Chisholm spoke to him sweetly. 'You know me, McCann. Did you say "Shamy" – is that our Indian friend?'

Terry abruptly hung up.

Chisholm turned to Arthur. 'What is it with you people? Don't you trust me?'

Back in the flat, Terry sat by the telephone, glaring at Shamy. 'We've gotta go . . . Twenty minutes and Chisholm's gonna be here.'

'But where're we going?'

'I don't know. Bombay?'

'Where'd I get the dough?'

'You're being dead straight, yeah? No moody . . . you're going to sell that video and come back with the money?'

'Course I will. I mean, them twenty pound notes – I was desperate.'

'Well, you're desperate now.'

'It's different –'

'It bloody is.' Terry went into the kitchen and fished out a plastic bag in the saucepan. As Terry rinsed the bag under the tap, he said. 'This is the best thing that's happened to me for six months. A Yankee – my first ever. Four winners on the trot. Punters like me dream about that.'

'How'd you pull that out?' asked Shamy.

'I just fancied them. Usually, I suss out the form, read the papers, horses for courses, who's the form jockey. But this time, I just *knew*.'

'Just luck then?' said Shamy disappointedly.

Terry arranged the notes on the draining-board. 'Well, don't knock it – it's going to get you out of an 'ole. You got your passport?'

'I'll phone her.' He picked up the telephone with a flourish. Hope had flowered again.

But not for long, for a saloon car was parked a few yards away from Shamy's flat. Two Indians sat in the front, with Mr Mitra in the back.

In Arthur's lock-up, chaos reigned as Chisholm searched, little caring for niceties. A disconsolate Arthur watched Chisholm tip over a tea-chest and spill the contents all over the floor. But there was nothing – no notes, no printing press. Meanwhile, Jones was prodding at a hardboard panel in the wall.

'This is a likely place, guv,' he said.

Eagerly Chisholm came over, picked up a large screwdriver and levered the panel.

'Just a bit of damp,' said Arthur casually.

'Could be a secret panel,' said Chisholm with manic delight.

'Nothing secret about it.'

'We might find all kinds of things here.' Chisholm was literally licking his lips in anticipation. He ripped off the panel and a small cloud of plaster and dust settled on his suit. As he shook off the dust, he said, 'As you said, Arthur – damp.

You'll have to have the builders in.' He flung the hardboard panel across the room.

'Charming,' Arthur muttered to himself.

'Eh, what d'you say?'

'Nothing.'

'I hope you're not questioning my behaviour?'

'The iron hand in a velvet glove. It's like having Attilla the Hun for tea.'

Then Arthur heard a strange sound from the yard – a kind of crunching and clanking that was reminiscent of a demented tractor. Hurrying, Arthur went to the door only to witness the return of the Daley School of Motoring car – dented, battered and with only one wing. Smudger stood beside it. A dazed Arthur slowly approached him.

'She's a nutter, y'know,' said Smudger. 'No question about it. She's a nutter.'

Chisholm was framed in the doorway. 'Not your day, Arthur,' he said smiling.

Terry's car approached the international terminal at Heathrow and he entered one of the multi-storey car-parks. Some way back at the roundabout, Gayle's car was being followed by Mr Mitra's saloon. A few minutes later, Gayle met Terry and Shamy as they waited beside the entrance to the tunnel that connected the car-park with the terminal building. She ran towards them, taking Shamy's passport from her handbag, and throwing her arms around him. Terry pushed them towards the tunnel and then began to run.

'You got everything?'

'Apart from the ticket –' Then to Shamy's horror, he saw Mr Mitra and his heavies approaching.

'You go ahead,' said Terry. 'I'll handle these guys.'

Shamy hesitated.

'Go on. This is my game – your game's running.' Terry looked around him. Then ahead he saw a long line of parked traffic trolleys. He darted for one of these, rolling it down the tunnel, while Shamy and Gayle ran into the terminal building. Terry wheeled another trolley down the tunnel and then another, until a barrage of wheels tore into Mitra and his gang. Mr Mitra fell over but a bolder Indian kicked away one of the trolleys and ran after Terry. He grabbed at him, Terry sidestepped, flinging his arms round the Indian's waist and depositing him into a trolley, rolling it down the tunnel so that it collided with Mr Mitra, just as he was painfully rising to his feet.

Back at the lock-up, Arthur was alone, sitting in the middle of the chaos like a broken-hearted clown. The telephone rang and he walked wearily to answer it.

'It's Terry – Shamy's on the plane to Bombay and Gayle's with me.'

'Good for you.'

'What's the matter, Arthur?'

'That Chisholm – he's a wicked man.

'You owe me money,' said Terry.

'I owe you money? What d'you mean – Bombay? I never said he could go. I wouldn't give him the fare to Bethnal Green.' Arthur hung up abruptly.

The next day, Syrup was to be seen on Arthur's lot, polishing the repaired 'learner' car. He was proudly wearing his new wig. Inside the caravan, Arthur said to Terry. 'He don't look like Roger Moore. Not in a million years.'

'He's thrilled to bits. He don't even mind if Chisholm nicks him.'

Then a taxi drew up by the car-lot. Gayle got out, saying something to the driver and walking quickly to the caravan.

'Hold on,' said Arthur, 'if she wants money, she's *your* friend.' He gave a gleaming smile to Gayle. 'Hallo, my darling – good news, like malaria or something?'

She slammed down a bulky envelope on the table.

'Yours. He cabled it and he's having a great time. He didn't get as much as he thought, but even so –'

'Why hasn't he come back?' asked Terry.

'He loves it so much that I'm going over as well. He's bought a ticket –'

'He said he'd be there for a day.'

'Yeah, but he reckons he likes it. Everything – the dust, the dirt, the heat and the squalor. It's magic. He's got a job –'

'That's the heat. It's affected his brain.'

'Anyway, there's two grand there and he said "thank you for everything". I've got to dash.' She quickly kissed Terry and went. Arthur stared at the contents of the envelope.

'Five hundred of that is mine,' said Terry slowly.

'And five hundred of it is also mine.'

'Then divi-up the rest –'

'I had all the aggravation –'

Outside, Chisholm had just parked his car. Syrup saw him and hid quickly behind a pile of oil drums. As Chisholm marched towards the caravan, Terry spotted and nudged Arthur who was counting out the money – in twenty pound notes. Arthur looked up, caught Chisholm's look of deep hatred and gave him a sickly smile.

PART FOUR

Terry walked across a vast graveyard of old cars, some of which were damaged or wrecked and others had just come to the end of their lives. Mounds of tyres, heaps of gearboxes and rotting hulks were piled on the ground, whilst looming above them were cranes, magnetic grabs, metal compressor machines – all the tools of the car breaking business.

Gypsy Joe was the boss here and he watched Terry come across his domain with all the pride of the king of a devastated country. At fifty, Joe was tough and wore a single ring in his right ear. While he was waiting for Terry he was prowling round the yard, seeing what he could rescue – be it a hub cap or a clutch pedal or a penny. Even now, Joe was poking into a heap of rubbish and picking up a Rover badge, dusting it and putting it into his dungaree pocket.

'Hi, Terry,' said Joe. 'I thought Arthur would come and see me personally.'

Terry smiled and handed over an envelope. 'He's expecting company.'

'Oh yeah,' said Joe, who had already opened the envelope and was counting the wad of twenty pound notes he found there.

'It's all there,' said Terry.

But Gypsy Joe wasn't going to stop counting. 'I can't read or write, but I can add and that's why I'm called the King of the Gypsies.'

'You don't still use that name, Joe? Gypsy?' said Terry cynically. 'I mean – you don't roam around a lot, do you?'

'Still got the caravan.'

'Yeah, I know,' said Terry. 'But its moored in the South of France, innit?'

'That's right,' replied Joe with a self-satisfied smirk. 'I've got it beside my villa.'

'That's what I mean. Don't reckon you're a raggle-taggle gypsy round the old camp fire any more.'

'Course not. I've got a nice house in Stanmore now and it's detached an' all,' he said proudly. 'But my heart is with my people, Terry – wherever they are.'

'Yeah,' said Terry drily, 'they've probably been evicted by the council, but obviously they can't have been evicted from Stanmore or you would have given them a nice site in your garden –'

'They can always ask me.' Gypsy Joe clapped Terry on the back. 'Let's go into the office.'

The office was a corrugated iron shed, highly ramshackle, caving in on the corner of the yard. As they passed a Mercedes Gypsy Joe pointed the car out. 'That's it,' he said.

'Not a lot of motor left,' said Terry.

'Nasty one – jumped over the barrier on the M4, right into a juggernaut.' Joe began to rummage through a pile of papers on his desk and finally he discovered the document he was searching for, which he put into an envelope. 'This is for Arthur. Vehicle document.'

'For what?' asked Terry.

'That one.' He pointed through the window to the wrecked Mercedes.

'He ain't buying that!' exclaimed Terry.

Joe smiled. 'I thought you were partners. He's putting in a "ringer" – a car from Germany; same make, different model. He's bound to make a handsome profit.'

'Haven't the insurance people told the Department of Transport?' asked Terry.

Joe said, 'You're a simple boy, Terry. Now the sad thing about that Mercedes is that the man forgot to post his premium. Some people are very unlucky – he broke five ribs and gawd knows what else and he got nicked for driving an uninsured vehicle. As it happens, I gave him a favour. Incidentally, Tel, if you ever see a write-off in your manor – you into a long 'un . . . just for commission.'

'Thanks,' replied Terry. 'I'll look round for any crippled drivers an' all.'

'They're like gold-dust.'

'Crippled drivers?' asked Terry.

'The vehicle documents,' explained Gypsy Joe patiently.

Terry went to the door. 'Yeah, sure. I'll see yer.'

'Wait a minute,' said Joe. 'You'll need the MOT certificate.'

Terry passed by the door, glancing down at the wrecked Mercedes. 'For that?'

'No – for the new one.'

'But, you haven't seen it.'

Joe looked at him righteously. 'Well I'm sure Arthur wouldn't sell a duff motor. It's trust – that's the name of the game in our business, Terry.'

Terry went out into the yard. 'Thanks,' he said, 'I'll remember that. It's a good word – trust.'

After his doubtful escapades in the Asian world, Arthur returned to more familiar territory on his second-hand car lot. He was expecting a ringer but he had time to spare for the odd punter. Directly he saw his unwary victim inspecting a Mini with a sticker on the windscreen saying, 'The Bargain of the Week', Arthur hurriedly walked over from his caravan office.

He began to peel off the sticker.

'Is it sold?' asked the punter immediately.

Arthur looked round as if he was surprised. 'Sorry, didn't see you, sir. Actually, my wife wants to buy it.' He gave a quick deprecating grin. 'No profit in it for me, eh? But there you go, if 'er indoors wants it – what can I do?' He paused. 'Were you interested in it, sir?'

'Well, I don't know. You reckon it's a good motor?'

'Good? Would I sell a vehicle to my own wife – or even to my own mother? No, this is one of the best. I had to go to the Duke of Norfolk's estate to buy that.'

'What – his own personal car?'

'Well, one hardly presumes that he's talking a lot of pork pies, is he?'

The punter was obviously impressed. 'Titled owner, eh?'

'Well,' said Arthur casually, 'he was wearing a deerstalker and a Harris tweed suit. I *assumed* that he was His Grace. We had a bit of conversation about horses. He's well into racing, as you probably know. Y'see, nice thing about the aristocracy is they like to keep their motors in good nick. Know what I mean?'

'He's probably got a garage,' said the punter naively.

'Well, he ain't going to park it outside his house, is he?'

The punter walked round the car. 'How much were you selling it for?'

'My wife would break her heart. Obviously, I was selling it to her for trade. Bad week for me.'

'How much did you say?'

'I didn't.'

'Oh.'

'I tell you what – I mean if you're interested, you are, aren't you?'

'Well, I –' his voice trailed off.

'Never mind "well". Her indoors set her heart on this little motor, given its pedigree. I'm a fool to myself – what with the financial climate and all that – I'll tell you what I'll do.' He clasped the punter's elbow and began to whisper confidentially.

MacFadyen, a hard forty-year old Scot, was driving a car transporter towards Arthur's car-lot. On board, the German Mercedes rocked gently – it was the ringer. But unfortunately, what MacFadyen didn't realise was that the nondescript van a few yards behind him contained two plain-clothed police officers, who were already reporting back to base the exact location of MacFadyen and his transporter.

'Rio Mary,' said one of the officers into a microphone, 'we've just picked him up – travelling eastward to Fulham.' But then the driver had to brake as a car ahead stopped for the red light.

'Sod it,' he said as MacFadyen's transporter jumped the lights.

A smiling Arthur was waving goodbye to the punter – and the Mini – when he saw MacFadyen parking his transporter. Arthur walked towards him. 'How're you doing, Frank?'

'Not so bad – and yourself?'

As MacFadyen climbed out of the cabin Arthur was

already looking at the cars on the back. 'Very handsome motors.'

'Great runners. In fact, my own wife wanted to buy the Merc, very clean car – too expensive for me.'

Arthur interrupted him. 'I've used that particular line this morning. Never lie to a liar, old son.'

MacFadyen grinned. 'I should've never said that to you. You're a bit too long in the tooth for that.'

'And they're all mine as well. Come on then – load off. I want to see this motor.'

MacFadyen started to lift down the ramp.

'Going up to Glasgow tomorrow?' asked Terry, emerging from the caravan with some new registration plates.

'Just going to relax here for a couple of days. I'm delivering the Porsche to a feller in Warren Street – have a few jars – maybe see my sister –'

'Nice motor. No problems?' asked Terry.

MacFadyen looked at him warily. 'Like what? Paid the customs and the tax. It's all down to Arthur now. If he's got the right logbook, it's a doddle for him. No come-backs if he's clever.'

'Oh, he's clever.'

'Would you like to come into the office?' said Arthur. 'Terry put them plates on.'

'How?' he asked simply.

'How? with a screwdriver – you have used a screwdriver before, haven't you? Documents – and put the right plate on the right motor.' He gave the documents to Terry and looked at MacFadyen. 'He's worse than two Irishmen.'

Terry said sarcastically, 'Have you got any tools in your workshop? I mean, things like screwdrivers, spanners, screws, bolts and nuts –'

'Now he's getting stroppy an' all. Go and borrow them.'

'No chance of actually buying them. Petty cash? A float?'

'Obviously, you'll be recompensed.'

'Yeah? I think I'll have a drink down the boozer instead. See you, Frank.' Abruptly, Terry left, exasperated, as usual, by Arthur's lies.

A few minutes later, Arthur was opening a briefcase stuffed with banknotes. He started counting with a bank clerk's expertise. 'That's the kind of problem we have in this country. Work? Where is he now – the honest English workman? He doesn't want to know about work. Graft? Not a chance. The sweat of the brow? No – it's all easy money now, the quick buck – as our American friends say. Years ago a man went to his workplace with a couple of slices of Hovis in his pocket and a nice piece of farmhouse cheese and he put in ten hours of honest toil. Now what do we get – luncheon vouchers! Sod it,' he said as he lost count. 'I'll have to start again now.' He licked his forefinger and rapidly began re-counting. 'What did we say? Seven grand?'

'I think we said seven grand five hundred and three hundred for the delivery charges.'

'You're more wicked than British Leyland,' said Arthur, as one professional to another.

Arthur would have been most agitated if he had realised that two Police Rovers were currently bearing down on him. In the second, Detective Sergeant Rycott sat with a large man named Inspector Klingmann, who had an impressive bearing and a hard intimidating scowl. He was an officer of the Federal Republic of Germany Police, on an exchange visit, an anglophile in tweeds, smoking a pipe. Beside him was Inspector Armstrong, middle-aged and sceptical.

As they neared Arthur's site, MacFadyen's car transporter drove past the police cars in the opposite direction. Then, as they pulled up beside the somewhat tatty-looking second-hand car display, the street became alive with policemen, plain-clothed men and uniformed officers. Police motor cycles stopped the traffic and a small crowd of curious onlookers began to gather.

Completely unaware of what was happening, Arthur was reading his newspaper when he looked up and saw Rycott approaching the hut. He smiled benignly, little realising that another officer was circling behind the caravan. Innocently, Arthur rose to welcome Rycott obsequiously, but an armed officer darted in front of him. 'Freeze!'

'Eh?'

'Keep your hands on the desk.'

Arthur saw Rycott standing behind him. Then he saw the full bastion of his armed colleagues. 'What's this then – a wind up?' But he was so surprised that he felt no other emotion but curiosity.

'You heard him. Hands on the desk.'

'It's me, Mr Rycott,' said Arthur, desperation replacing his curiosity.

'I know who you are.'

'Well, what's all this business. "Freeze?" It's Starsky and Crutch –'

'Do as you're told.'

Arthur then finally realised that Rycott was in earnest and he put up his hands. 'Can I ask why?'

'Shurrup,' said the armed officer.

'Am I being arrested?'

'Course not. We just want to talk to you –'

'Like this?'

'Down the road.'

'In the nick, you mean? Certainly not –'

Rycott gave him a wolfish grin. 'Okay, then do a runner. You wouldn't get to the pavement. There's ten armed coppers surrounding this place. At least one of them's gun-happy – got to be. Fancy your chances?'

Arthur stared at him in bewilderment. 'But what've I done? I mean, just give me a hint?'

'All in good time, Arthur,' said Rycott patiently. 'Now are you coming quietly?'

Outside Klingmann and Inspector Armstrong were looking at the gleaming Merc. They had opened the bonnet and seemed interested in the engine.

Klingmann glanced up as Arthur was escorted by two armed officers to a police car. Arthur mustered as much dignity as he could – given the fact that one of the officers was shoving him into the car.

When Terry returned from the pub, carrying a couple of screwdrivers and spanners, he discovered the Merc being lifted up on to a police break-down trailer. There were policemen still nosing around the site, whilst two uniformed constables were telling curious onlookers to keep moving.

Terry paused and crossed to the other side of the road. There was no sign of Arthur.

At the police station a shirtsleeved officer was about to take Arthur's fingerprints.

'Eh, eh – just a minute. I'm not having my dabs –'

'Why?'

'Why? Because I have certain rights.'

'They always say that.'

'I don't care about that.' Arthur was insistent. 'I still don't know why I'm in here.'

The officer wrestled gently with Arthur's hand. 'Well, I don't know, do I? Take his dabs – that's all they said to me. I mean, we've got to distinguish you from the other suspects.'

'What suspects?'

'I don't know, do I? Anyway – everybody should have his fingerprints. I mean, say you fell into the river and you lost your wallet. Drowned. Stone dead. How could we identify you? We're not talking about crime; we're talking about personal identity.'

'I never go near the river.'

'Car crash? Collapse in the street? I mean, it's common sense. I'm a great believer in identity.' He still continued taking Arthur's prints. 'We've got to sort out the goats from the sheep, eh?' he said, as if he was talking to a patient. 'Painless, innit?'

'Yeah, I know,' said Arthur caustically. 'You've got them, anyway.'

'Really? I'd have thought that you'd never been in a police station before. Tissue?' He offered a Kleenex box. 'Years ago we never had things like this – a dirty old rag. Hygiene – see? That's the thing these days. Sit down over there, sir.'

Arthur sat down on a bench. A few minutes later, another officer passed him and said, 'Don't sit there. Go over there –'

Arthur crossed to a chair by the corner. Then he called out to his retreating back. 'Excuse me! Could you please tell me what this is all about?'

'No idea, mister,' said the officer, without pausing.

Arthur fidgeted and clicked his teeth. Various police officers walked about the area, each looking purposeful and businesslike. Then another officer passed. 'I say, could I just ask –'

'I'm busy.'

'Oh, thanks,' Arthur said as the officer disappeared down the corridor. 'That's great, innit? The one time you need one they're all busy,' he muttered to himself. After a while, he peeped round the corner to see Rycott approaching. Arthur rose quickly.

'Mr Rycott, can I have a quick word?'

'No.' He was carrying a file.

'I can't have that. I am a law-abiding ratepayer –'

'Who says?'

'I'll ignore that. But as nobody knows why I'm here, do you think I can go now?'

'You must be joking? You're helping the police. You know, "a man is being interviewed by the local police." That man is you.'

Arthur stared at him. 'In that case I think I should phone my solicitor.'

'Why'

'Why? Are you cognizant of the common law of this country? Magna Carta – and all that? Habeas corpus, the inalienable right of decent Englishmen? May I suggest that you are well out of order, Mr Rycott?'

Rycott started to say something, but Arthur hurriedly continued.

'I haven't finished yet. When my brief comes down here *he* is going to give you and your superiors a right verbal thrashing –'

'Yeah, yeah, yeah – OK. What's his name?'

'Ivan Silkman, of –'

'You're kidding. He's doing eighteen months in Ford Open nick.'

'That's his brother, a headstrong lad,' said Arthur quickly. 'But Ivan is one of the rising lights in the legal profession.'

'I'll give him a bell,' said Rycott grudgingly.

'And quick.'

Rycott scowled and started down the corridor.

Arthur's complaining voice pursued him. 'I think I've been very decent to you people. I mean, fair's fair – but you haven't even suggested what the charge is.'

Rycott turned. 'We're working on it.'

'Like what?'

'I don't know – conspiracy maybe.'

'You what?' Arthur sounded shocked.

'Harbouring, illegal substances –? Smuggling drugs? Causing a riot? Oh and – that German motor hasn't got a MOT certificate – not a real one at least.' Rycott walked away, whilst Arthur looked dumbfounded. For a moment he didn't realise that another officer, this time the gaoler, was shepherding him towards a door.

'This way, please . . . sir.'

'Yeah,' he said absentmindedly. But it was not until he was walking down the white tiled corridor that Arthur realised where they were heading. 'Hey, what's going on?'

The gaoler lead him towards a cell. 'You'll be all right here, sir.'

Arthur began to pant. 'That's a cell.'

'Quite harmless. Excuse me.' He began to pull off Arthur's tie. 'And these, sir.' He undid Arthur's braces.

'Gawd help us,' said Arthur grabbing at his trousers.

'You'll be better in there. It's all hurry and scurry upstairs, you can't even hear yourself think . . . what with coppers running around and people being arrested, shouting and swearing. This is much nicer.' He smiled generously. 'You only have to knock if you want anything, sir.' With that he slammed the door closed, leaving Arthur a shocked, shuddering heap.

Arthur's Mercedes was being systematically dismantled. The doors had been removed and the bonnet. The car was on a hydraulic ramp with two mechanics busy removing the exhaust system. A plain-clothed officer was discussing progress with the shop foreman.

'Are you going to be able to put it all back together?' he asked jocularly.

'The Jerries can do it; why not us?' said the foreman. 'Incidentally, the shock absorbers are a bit iffy.'

'I don't want to buy it, Charlie. Let's just find the stuff, right?'

In Warren Street, the second-hand car market of London, MacFadyen was unloading a Porsche from his transporter. When it was finally set on the roadway a car dealer called Ronnie slid into the driving seat with MacFadyen beside him. Ronnie was very flash, with a chunky gold bracelet, half a ton of gold watch on the other wrist and a Dior gold tooth-pick dangling on his solarium-tanned chest.

Ronnie tried to back the Porsche into his garage-cum-showroom, but it was a tricky manoeuvre which annoyed him, for he liked to show off his driving. As he started the car backwards, he brushed an old parked car and swore. But when he saw MacFadyen grinning he laughed and said, 'That was nothing, believe me. Just a little scratch. He shouldn't have parked here anyway – this is for people in the trade.' He glanced around him. 'I know every car in the street and that wreck is a stranger. Probably a punter,' said Ronnie as he switched off the ignition.

'I'll have a wee look, just the same,' said MacFadyen suspiciously.

Ronnie squeezed MacFadyen's shoulder 'I'll tell you what. This isn't a bad motor. You know I drove a lot.'

'I can see that,' said MacFadyen with a straight face.

'Do a bit of rallying, know what I mean?'

'Is that right?'

'Yeah. I'm a member of The DrivingWheel Club – Jackie Stewart, Fittipaldi, the new French feller – I met 'em all.' He glanced round the interior of the car. 'Nice and clean, isn't it?' He pushed the stereo button on the radio. 'Nice music.' Ronnie got out and prowled around the car looking at the bumper. 'Told you – not a scratch. Hard to sell a motor in Glasgow.'

'Aye, but we're in London, aren't we?' said MacFadyen. 'Anyway, I've got a punter in Glasgow. A decent guy – managing director of a building business.'

Ronnie nodded making it clear that he'd heard it all before. 'Yeah – managing director – they all say that.' He gave a quick grin. 'No disrespect to you. Now, you were hoping to get ten and a half for this, weren't you?'

'That's what we said on the phone.'

'Yeah, I know, but now I see the actual motor –'

MacFadyen interrupted him, looking particularly evil. 'Don't piss me around – I did all the work and I've got contacts over there. They've even changed the number on the chassis and the engine. You've got to realise, German villains are very efficient. All you've got to do is stand by the corner and cop five grand for just wearing out your shoe leather.'

Ronnie gave him a cynical grin. 'As it happens, I'm hoping to get about eight grand. I like very, very expensive shoes, Frank.'

Terry walked into the solicitor's office and was immediately rebuffed by Karen, the receptionist. 'Sorry, we're closed now, love.'

'It's an emergency,' said Terry dourly.

'Oh, it's you, Terry. You in trouble or something?'

'No. Is he in?'

'He's gone shooting for the weekend. It's his new thing – he's gone right off golf. I think it's because he mixes with a lot of people who like shooting – robbers, you know what I mean?'

'Yeah,' said Terry. 'Have you got his number?'

'He doesn't want to be disturbed.'

'This is important – Arthur's in the nick.'

'Well, he's certainly not interested in Arthur. We haven't

had his last cheque yet or the one before.'

'Must have slipped his mind,' said Terry.

'I bet.'

'This is an emergency,' said Terry.

'You've already told me –' The telephone rang and Karen picked up the receiver. 'Sorry, he's gone for the weekend. Oh, hallo Sergeant Rycott –'

'Just a minute,' said Terry, 'let me talk to him.'

Hesitantly, Karen gave the phone to Terry.

'Mr Rycott?'

'Yes, Terry?'

'What's the SP on Arthur?'

'He's just helping us with our enquiries.'

'But what's the charge?:'

'Nothing yet – but there will be.'

'Will he be appearing in court?'

'If I've got anything to do with it,' said Rycott, 'he'll be in the Magistrates' Court on Monday.'

'Can I have him out on bail?' asked Terry.

'No chance – he's here for the weekend, while we pursue our enquiries. He wanted his solicitor.'

'Yeah,' said Terry, 'but he's not around, he's gone shooting.'

'That's nice,' said Rycott.

'Could I see him?'

'If you find out where he's shooting.'

'No,' said Terry patiently. 'I mean Arthur.'

'Maybe.'

'What do you mean, maybe, Sergeant Rycott?'

'What I say.'

'But look – if he hasn't got his solicitor there –'

'Listen Terry, said Sergeant Rycott, 'are you suggesting I'm not doing things by the book?'

'No, Mr Rycott. Not in the least. But I would like to see him.'

'Come down here and chance your luck,' said Rycott. 'If we've got time you might be able to drop into his cell for five minutes.'

Terry put down the phone and turned back to Karen. 'We're in stuk. Can't you possibly give me that phone number?'

'Sorry,' said Karen. 'And if you see Arthur, give him this envelope.'

'What's in it?' said Terry.

'His prior account.'

'Please help me.'

'I told you – Ivan needs his rest just as much as anyone else. Why don't you go down to the Law Centre?'

'That's for squatters and old ladies who are being evicted,' said Terry.

Karen closed her handbag primly. 'You do understand that there's one law for everybody, don't you?'

In the police station that was currently housing Arthur, Klingmann and Inspector Armstrong were studying a file, while Rycott looked on.

'Not guilty. Not guilty. Not guilty.' Klingmann's very correct English accent was beginning to show frustration. 'Excuse me, but do you ever convict people like this?'

'Well, he's a slippery character, Daley.'

'Slippery?'

'I think the Sergeant means that Daley is a very clever criminal,' said Armstrong.

'Obviously – I see here that he had a sentence for eighteen months, twenty-four years ago.'

Rycott looked over his shoulder. 'He had a couple of parking offences three years ago,' he said with a hopeful smile. 'You see, when I heard about it, I thought, well, it's not Arthur's usual game.'

'Sergeant, I want you to assist Inspector Klingmann in every way,' said Inspector Armstrong.

'Yessir.'

'This is an Anglo-German operation. So I want you to explain Daley's "usual game".'

Rycott began to speak slowly and carefully. 'Well, I mean – he's a rascal, no question about it. He's a scallywag – but, I can't buy Arthur, I mean, Daley, as a drug dealer. For a start, it's dangerous.'

'That is because the stakes are high.'

'But he's a devout coward, sir. A dodgy motor, yes. But –'

Klingmann was annoyed. 'I have had very reliable sources and efficient methods.'

'In that case, why didn't you intercept the car in Germany?' asked Armstrong with a smile.

'Nobody is perfect, you know,' he snapped. 'Including here . . . Not guilty, not guilty, not guilty. What is the expression here? This man is overdue, yes?'

'Well overdue, sir.'

'And talking about overdue. I should be at a Police Federation meeting in a few minutes,' put in Armstrong.

'Another rise, sir?'

'In the pipeline, I think.'

Klingmann looked at them incredulously.

'Rycott will help you in every way, Inspector,' said Armstrong as he hurriedly departed.

'Well, how about a nice cup of tea, sir?' asked Rycott cheerfully.

'I do not wish tea. I would rather meet Mister Daley.' He paused. 'Unless he is already having some tea.'

Rycott smiled weakly. 'I'll wheel him in, sir.'

Arthur sat down in front of the desk gloomily. Rycott had just told him that they were unable to contact his solicitor because he was away – which left him feeling properly high and dry. There was a long pause whilst Klingmann studied some documents. The only light in the room was from a desk lamp. Arthur smiled hopefully and Klingmann looked up.

'Not guilty, eh?' he said with a sour smile.

'I beg your pardon?'

'Nothing. Do you smoke?' Klingmann offered him a pack of cigarettes although he was puffing a pipe himself.

'Cigar man. But they didn't leave my matches.' He gave a sideways glance at Rycott. 'Or me braces.'

'Go ahead,' said Klingmann.

Arthur took out a cigar, offering one to Klingmann who declined. Then the officer struck him a match.

'Apparently you have many friends in Germany?' asked Klingmann.

Arthur was still lighting his cigar. 'Never been to the place.' He straightened up. 'Is this about the motor? I am a bona fide motor trader. And anybody knows that I'm –'

'You are giving me answers and I haven't even given the questions yet.'

'Sorry – I'm usually quick, see.'

'Oh, yes, I realise that. Any man with your history of "not guilty's," I have to respect.'

Arthur gave him a strained smile and said, 'Am I assuming that I am talking to a German police officer?'

'This is true.'

'Charming.' He looked at Rycott. 'This is all down to the Common Market, innit? I mean – me – *me*, interrogated by a German. And they know a lot about interrogating, don't they?'

'Don't be cheeky, Arthur,' said Rycott firmly. 'He's just asking some questions.

'It's like Colditz.'

'Listen, any more of that and I'm going to nick you under the Race Relations Act –'

'That's for Lucozades – not for Jerries.'

'We're all brothers under the skin these days, Arthur.' Rycott turned to Klingmann. 'Sorry, Inspector.'

'Thank you. I repeat, who are your contacts in Germany?'

'I've told you. Just a simple car dealer, C of E, free enterprise – a true patriot. I was in the British Army, you know, King and Empire. I mean, Queen and Commonwealth.'

'All right, Arthur – we've got all your previous.'

'Who are the people you bought the car from?' asked Klingmann.

Arthur relaxed. 'That's easy – Old Frank.'

'Who?'

Arthur looked worried again. 'His name's Frank – I mean,

in my game it's all down to cash and first names. Everybody knows that. Got it – a receipt, no problem.' Searching in his pockets, Arthur found the receipt which looked indecipherable. 'Well, it's Frank – Frank somebody or other. There's a "M" there. "Mac" something. I don't know.'

Klingmann looked at the receipt and then gave it to Rycott.

'The tax people will like that. Are all your transactions like these?'

'That's down to my accountant, innit. He keeps meticulous books –'

'I hope you can remember *his* name.'

'Obviously. You see this name, this Frank. I can't understand his writing. I mean, they're not all that clever with writing and things, I mean, your Scotsmen. A bit handy with the roll-call and putting in the head and that's it.'

Klingmann stared stonily at him. Rycott smiled.

'My old mum is from Scotland.'

'I mean some of them. Old Frank – just an ordinary bloke, not your actual scholar. Can I see it again?' He paused.

Rycott gave him the scrap of paper.

'See that first name, Frank – that's quite clear. It's the other name, right? Mac – innit?'

'Mac – what?'

'I don't know – they've all got Mac's up there, haven't they?' He smiled. 'Got it – he came on the boat. Well, the passport people – they check all the names. That's your answer – documents. You people like that,' he said to Klingmann. Then he returned to Rycott and said, 'They love documents – Germans.'

'I don't care about the documents! I want to find out what's *in* the car. Drugs!' said Klingmann angrily.

'Drugs!'

'Narcotics.'

'I'm not into that. What do you think I am? The Fulham connection?'

'Why not?'

'Mr Rycott – tell him? Arthur Daley – a drug fiend? I don't

even trust one of them Paracetamols.'

'You could be a middle man though.'

Rycott grinned for he was enjoying this interrogation.

Arthur stared at both of them dazedly. 'That's it then. I don't say another word without my solicitor here.'

'I told you – he's gone shooting.'

'Then, I'm going.'

'Give us a chance, Arthur. This is a serious case. I thought you'd help us.'

'Of course I would. The man you're after is Frank What's-'is-name.'

'And we'll get him,' said Rycott. 'But in the meantime, I'd be grateful if you could dwell here for a while –'

'That's right – always help your local sheriff – correct, yes?' He beamed at his own heavy humour whilst Arthur glanced warily at Rycott.

MacFadyen was pouring champagne in a drinking club and clinking glasses with Ronnie, the second-hand car salesman, and Rita, who was young and sexy.

'To you, Rita,' said MacFadyen.

'Isn't he nice. I love your accent, Frank.'

'And I love your pretty face and your beautiful figure,' said MacFadyen leering. 'I bet you're a dancer.'

'You're right.'

'You was in the Royal Ballet, wasn't you?'

'Only for a bit,' she said. 'They're very stuck up, some of them. So I went to Tunisia with a group and that was more like modern dancing.'

'Ready for another one, Frank?'

'It's my shout,' said MacFadyen. 'Rita, do you fancy any more of the old bubbly?'

'Why not?' said Rita.

MacFadyen drunkenly lurched towards the small bar and Ronnie said to Rita, 'It's about time we got a bit busy on him, darling. He's got ten grand in his bin and that was only from me. Gawd knows how much more he's got on him, and he sold a nice Merc an' all.'

'Yeah, but I don't want him in my place,' said Rita.

'Course not – you gotta box clever. Take him to a hotel – George's gaff – he'll let anybody in; all the brasses use it.'

'Don't you call me a bloody brass,' said Rita indignantly.

'Course you're not,' replied Ronnie ingratiatingly. 'You're just in between engagements. Like between Swan Lake and the go-go at Marrakesh.'

Arthur lay miserably on his cot in the cell, with his shirt sleeves rolled up, whilst a doctor tested his blood pressure. He looked carefully down at the instrument as he unrolled the band around Arthur's arm.

'Well?' asked Arthur anxiously.

'You're fine.'

'Are you sure, doc?'

'Nothing wrong with you. You're as sound as a bell.'

'It can't be,' said Arthur disappointedly. 'I had a kind of turn.'

'What kind of turn?' asked the doctor.

'Well, I felt sort of dizzy like, with palpitations and apart from that, I suffer from claustrophobia –'

'Well,' said the doctor, with an ironic smile, 'this really isn't the place to be if you suffer from claustrophobia.'

'I told them,' said Arthur. 'I'm a nervous wreck. Usually I can have a nap anywhere. Not here.'

'Don't worry about it,' said the doctor. 'I'll give a tablet to the gaoler.'

'Don't give one to him,' said Arthur. 'I'm the one who needs it.'

But the doctor gave him a patient look. 'I'll give it to him and he'll give it to you. Do you understand that?'

'Yeah,' said Arthur.

'Goodnight.' Then the doctor went out and the gaoler appeared, telling Arthur that he had a visitor.

'About time an' all,' said Arthur picking up his jacket and walking behind the gaoler to an interview room in the station where Terry was sitting at a table.

'Where have you been?' asked Arthur.

'Well, give us a chance.'

'Why? I'm cooped up in here. Where's Ivan?'

'He's gone –'

'Yes,' said Arthur interrupting wrily, 'I know, he's gone shooting. But why?'

'I don't know,' replied Terry. 'Maybe he's joining the Israeli army. Why don't you sit down?'

'I will,' said Arthur and scowled at the officer who lounged beside the door.

After a pause, Terry said, 'It's a turn-up, innit?'

Arthur stared at him. 'Is that all you can say, when I'm in a situation like this, without a tie and no braces. I mean – I can understand prison riots now. I'm not kidding you – I'm stir crazy.'

'You've only been here for five hours,' said Terry.

'But it's the principle, isn't it. I'm a free spirit. I miss the buses.'

'What?'

'I miss the buses. I don't know why, but I have an obsession with red buses.'

'I think you're pregnant,' said Terry.

'Listen, Terry. This is a very big case. You do realise the Germans are after me, don't you?'

'What do you mean?'

'You know what they're like. Fulham today and brave little Belgium tomorrow.'

'Look – it's a simple case of mistaken identity,' said Terry.

'So was the case of the Count of Monte Cristo,' replied Arthur, 'and what about 'er indoors. What's she gonna say when she comes back from her sister's? The local paper will have a bonanza when they start putting up the headlines about a well known public figure in pokey. You've got to remember that my kids go to a private school and they mingle with scions of local personalities.'

'What about the stockbroker who's doing plenty of bird?' asked Terry.

'That's not the same,' said Arthur. 'That was business, not crime. Their talking about me as the mastermind of the

Fulham connection. And that's what happens when you do business with Scotchmen.'

'You were happy enough when you were stitching him up,' said Terry.

'Stitching him up!' exclaimed Arthur. 'Be fair, Tel – I was doing an honest deal. You do a favour – and then what? I had a feeling in my water with that man.'

'MacFadyen? Seemed a decent guy.'

'What? Give me the guy's name.'

'MacFadyen,' said Terry.

'MacFadyen, that's manna from heaven.' Arthur looked as if he was going to burst into tears. 'Why didn't you tell me before?'

'I've only been here a few minutes,' said Terry.

Arthur addressed the officer leaning against the door. 'Did you get that?'

'Eh?'

'Listen, officer. You're supposed to listen to our conversation. Did you get that name?'

'I wasn't listening.'

'Terrific, eh?' said Arthur to Terry. 'Anyway, I'll tell Rycott now that I've got the name.'

'Maybe I'll have a quick creep down Warren Street,' said Terry.

'Why?'

''Cause he had a Porsche on the back of his trailer and I know he was going down there.'

'Blimey,' said Arthur, impressed. 'Full marks for observation. You really amaze me – not a lot, but just sometimes. Now get down there,' said Arthur theatrically. 'Find that man.'

'What about Rycott, the pride of the force?'

'Him,' said Arthur scornfully, 'he couldn't find a tart in a brothel.'

Terry walked down Warren Street, scrutinising the cars and rather crumby showrooms and garages. Dealers were chatting on every corner and the cars were parked bumper to bumper. Terry spotted the Porsche almost at once, jutting out from a garage entrance with a mechanic fitting a new registration number plate. Terry crossed the street and asked him, 'Guv'nor around?'

But Ronnie, hopefully spotting a punter, was already by his side. 'Handsome motor, eh?'

'Yeah.'

'You trade?'

'Sort of.'

'What's that mean?' asked Ronnie with a phoney smile.

'Always interested in an imported car from Germany.'

'What's that mean?' said Ronnie.

'You said that before,' said Terry with a grin.

'Who are you then?' asked Ronnie impatiently. 'VAT man?'

'No.' Then Terry spoke pleasantly. 'You met a feller from Glasgow yesterday –'

'What's it to you? I don't know nothing about the guy. I buy 'em and sell 'em. OK. See yer.' He turned away, walking back to his office, but Terry grabbed his arm.

'Just a minute – you're not being very nice, are you?'

'If you don't let go of my arm, you'll be asking for a slap.'

'Leave it out,' said Terry still smiling, but Ronnie swung at him and Terry grabbed the other wrist, pulling him towards the car.

'I don't know nothing about the guy,' Ronnie shouted. 'I just had a drink with him.'

'You know more than that.'

Ronnie turned to his mechanic. 'Gary, sort him out.'

But the mechanic wasn't having any. 'I clean 'em, you sell 'em – you sort him out.'

Ronnie tried to relinquish Terry's grip, but he wasn't strong enough and Terry pushed his face under the open bonnet. 'Come on, you're not helping me, are you?'

'Push off.'

'Nice clean engine –'

'Okay, it wasn't down to me. He went away with a brass.'

'Where?'

'Hotel in King's Cross.'
'What's it called?'
'Nero's Palace.'
Terry released him and Ronnie staggered back.
'Thanks,' said Terry.
Ronnie aimed a wild swing at him but Terry easily swayed out of distance. 'You should be nicer to people,' said Terry.

Back in the police repair shop various parts of the Mercedes were littered around the floor and the seats were propped up against a wall. A plain clothed man wandered into the shop and walked up to the foreman.
'Find anything?'
'Nothing.'
'What about the sump?'
'There wasn't even any oil in it – never mind drugs,' said the foreman sourly. 'But now we've come across a real problem.'
'What's that?'
'We're on double time.'
'Tell your guv'nor.' The plain clothed policeman walked slowly away.

When Terry stepped into the tatty reception area of Nero's Palace, Georgie, the obese owner, was having a cup of tea and checking his accounts.
'Yessir?'
'Looking for one of your guests. Mr MacFadyen?'
'That's a new one.'
'It probably is in here. Scotch? Tall. About forty.'
'Who are you? Old Bill?'
'I'm just a mate of his.'
'I've got a lot of residents.'
'He came in with a – you know – his wife.'
'I don't want a big party. The other two guys have already –' But he never finished the sentence for pandemonium suddenly broke out upstairs. 'Bloody hell,' said Georgie.
There was shouting, screams and the crashing of breaking

furniture. It was the latter sound that made Georgie, despite his weight, begin to ascend the stairs at a considerable speed. He was closely followed by Terry. But directly Georgie and Terry reached the landing, a door was wrenched open on the next floor and MacFadyen began to take the stairs, two at a time.

'Frank –' said Terry conversationally, as MacFadyen shoved Georgie aside. Then he hit Terry flush on the chin and Terry collapsed to the floor, whilst MacFadyen ran to the exit.

A few seconds later, Terry sat up against the wall, ruefully massaging his jaw.

'I thought you were a mate of his?' said Georgie.

'More like nodding acquaintances really.' Terry rose shakily to his feet, while, at the same time, two heavies, dishevelled and with multiple abrasions, stumbled from the room. One of them glanced at Terry and Georgie as they passed. 'Bloody nutters. All them Jocks are nutters,' he said.

When Terry and Georgie entered the room a girl lay naked in a disarrayed bed. The room was a shambles and she was fingering a nasty bruise on her cheek.

'Get your clothes on,' said Georgie. 'I run a respectable hotel.'

'I knew you'd say that,' she remarked sarcastically.

'That's right. I mean, this is a family hotel.'

'Don't give me all that crap. You run a glorified knocking shop.' She glanced at Terry. 'Who the hell is this?'

'I'm the man from the Michelin Guide,' said Terry.

'What're you going to give – a rosette or crossed fists?'

Terry picked up MacFadyen's hold-all.

'Nothing in there,' she said, but he had already found a tattered address book. 'I'm looking for his sister's address.'

'What's she? Female wrestler?' She took a cigarette and lit it, whilst Georgie rearranged the furniture. 'He had his money in his socks. No wonder he kept them on.'

'You're lucky. My pal's in the nick because of him.'

'Tough titty. He never even paid me. All I got was a right-hander.' With a touch of dignity she tidied the bedclothes. 'I don't usually do this, you know.'

'And what about the two creepers –?'

'Not my friends.' She gave a meaningful glance. 'Were they, Georgie? They were after something he had.'

'You'd better go. Come on,' said Georgie.

'Don't talk to me like that,' shouted Rita. Despite her toughness, she was nearly in tears. 'He paid the room in advance. Blimey, with all this I'm due early morning tea and biccies.'

Terry pocketed the address book.

She eyed Terry. 'I don't suppose you're interested in a bit of business?'

'Not really,' said Terry unbelievingly. 'But I'll give you that – you're a trier! See you.' He went to the door quickly.

Arthur lay on his bunk, staring at the ceiling. He didn't even react to the sound of the lock rattling. The door opened and the gaoler ushered in Billy North, known as The Ferret. He was short, skinny and shifty.

'Sorry, sir,' said the gaoler absentmindedly to Arthur, 'busy night.' He slammed the door.

'Oh, my Gawd –' said Arthur.

'Arthur Daley! This is a real privilege – I mean – Arthur Daley!'

'Don't give me all that. You are privileged, as it happens. But I know *why!* Of all people – The Ferret!'

'I hate that name,' Billy said disappointedly. 'Why do they call me that?'

'Ever had a look in the mirror?'

'You can depend on me, Arthur.'

'You? You've got more grass than Kew Gardens.'

'Me, Arthur? Never. On my mother's eyesight.'

'She's dead. I was at the funeral nine years ago. And you – you wasn't even there.'

'They wouldn't let me out. I did a runner when me dad was buried. Can I sit down, Arthur?'

'No. Go and sit somewhere else.'

Unconcerned by the insult Billy sat on the floor. 'I had a

nice one tonight – jeweller's shop. Do you know, I got arrested by a dog.'

Arthur stared at him. 'On his own?'

'Clever, ain't they? Three law – but it was due to the dog.'

Arthur shook his head wonderingly. 'You're just a simple recidivist.'

'I'm inadequate – that's what they said.'

'Well, don't be so proud about it.'

'I'm just telling you what they said. I'm surprised to see you here.'

Immediately Arthur was alert. 'Well, here I am,' he said sourly.

'I've always respected you, Arthur,' Billy said ingratiatingly.

'Yeah?'

'You're a well respected man in the manor. Hard though.'

'Yeah.'

'Oh, no doubt about it – a hard man in business. Everybody knows that. That's why you've gone a long way –'

Despite himself, Arthur smiled. 'Very true, Ferret. I mean – Billy.'

'Don't get me wrong when I say "hard", not physical. I mean, you've got Terry and he's as hard as you can get.'

'Where was he when I needed him?' he muttered.

'What was that?'

'Nothing.'

'That's what I thought.'

'Eh?'

'You don't think that Terry's done something – well, you know – he hasn't put you in this spot of bother?'

Arthur sat up slowly and stared at the Ferret. 'Who told you to say that?' he asked softly with creeping suspicion.

'Oh, no –' He was beginning to look shifty.

Arthur stared at him with an expression of complete revulsion. 'You never concocted that theory all on your own,' he said menacingly.

Billy gave a guilty smile. 'I don't know what you mean.'

'As you say, I'm not a physical person, Ferret. Brain rather than brawn. But in your case, I could make an exception.'

Billy, who was only half Arthur's size, gave him a sickly smile. 'Sorry – no offence, Arthur.'

Arthur put on an assumed drawl. 'Don't mess with me, Ferret.' A little power was a good thing, he thought, particularly after he had just avoided a real stitch-up.

Terry stood outside the nurses' home, watching them bustling in and out. Then, taking courage in both hands, he approached a blonde nurse.

'Hallo. D'you know Bridget MacFadyen?'

'I might do.'

'Is she around?'

'Where did she find you?' asked the nurse grinning.

'I'm the phantom lurker.'

'I've been looking for you for years,' she said amidst the giggles of others.

'Can I get you on the National Health?' said Terry.

'All free,' said the nurse. 'Come with me.'

'Why?' said Terry cautiously.

'Because, you'll never get past security. Just follow me.' She took him round to a fire escape and pointed upwards. 'Be lucky,' she said with a smile. 'MacFadyen's in number 27.'

'Bless you,' said Terry as he went up the stairs.

Knocking quietly on the door of number twenty-seven, Terry waited hesitantly, not knowing how he was going to play it. Then the door was opened by a large and attractive girl with a mild Glasgow accent.

'You must be Bridget,' he said.

'What's it to you?'

'I'm a friend of Frank's.'

'Is there something wrong?' she asked alarmed.

'Not really, but could I come in for a minute?'

'That might be dodgy – you might be the rapist.'

'I promise I'm not.'

'Anyway, I can look after myself. You had better come in.'

She opened the door and he entered the tiny room. 'What's wrong?' she asked. 'I only talked to him twenty minutes ago.'

'I just left him,' said Terry.

'Then why did he give you my address?'

'It's a long story,' said Terry. 'Can I sit down?'

But suddenly, Bridget was both alarmed and suspicious. 'I don't believe he gave you my address.'

'All right then – I found it.'

'Get out.'

'Now, don't start screaming,' he said, but before he could finish the sentence, she had rushed for the door. 'I'm not going to hurt you,' said Terry. But to his surprise she did not scream, but punched him in the face. She shaped up like a real fighter as Terry side-stepped. 'Give us a chance,' said Terry as he ducked another blow. 'Where do you work out?' he asked her as she tried to knee him in the groin. 'Don't do that,' he said and grabbed her, putting her into a clinch.

'I'll scream,' she said.

'Not you,' replied Terry and pushed her away so that she stumbled into the other wall. 'You're never going to be raped, are you?'

But Bridget was ready to fight again. 'Only if you want to,' she said.

'Take a standing count,' shouted Terry. 'A friend of mine is in trouble and Frank can help him. That's why I've come.'

Bridget poised, ready to dart at him again, but this time she was listening.

'This pal – he bought a car from Frank, but now the police want to nick him.'

'Are you a copper?' asked Bridget with returned suspicion.

'No, I'm not. But for all I know, they're after your brother.'

'He's done nothing,' said Bridget quickly.

'How d'you know?' protested Terry. 'You don't know what it's all about yet.'

'My brother's a decent man.'

'I'm sure he is, but I've got to see him and all I'm asking is how to. Will you help me?'

'I might,' she said.

'It's important – honest it is. I mean, I'm not going to hurt him. Anyway, he can take care of himself – I'm sure it runs in the family.'

Bridget deliberated for a while and then she said, 'All right – I'll show you where to find him.'

Terry and Bridget walked down the street together.

'Have you lived here long?' asked Terry.

'About a year. I'd had enough of Glasgow.' She paused. 'Lived in Brixton for a week and the riots started. It was worse than Parkhead, so I got a job around here.'

'It's all right around here.'

'I've always been a great fan of Chelsea. Mind you, I don't like the colours. I support Celtic. I've met a lot of players at the hospital. It's handy for them – you know, the hospital what with their injuries and whatever –'

'In Fulham the players haven't even got a first aid box. A couple of corn plasters and that's it.'

'Where did you learn boxing?'

'Here and there. And you?'

Bridget scowled and Terry grinned to cover up. 'Don't hit me.'

They crossed the road, heading towards a pub.

'I'm the only girl out of a family of six.' She smiled. 'The survival of the fittest. By the time I was fifteen, I was punchy. The left jab isn't bad.'

'I've seen worse.'

'Now I'm a lover – not a fighter.'

Terry appraised her fine figure. 'A bit like myself.'

'Is that right?' She paused. 'I bet you like little, slim girls who drink German wine.'

'I don't know about that. And what about the fellers you like? Eighteen stone, bullworker muscles and a convertible Roller.'

'No.' She paused. 'You'll do,' she said smiling. 'I've got an awful thirst – I could murder a pint of Export.'

'Are you going to strangle it? Only kidding, Bridget,' he said quickly, opening the door of the pub.

In the police repair shop, the Mercedes was now totally dismantled – with wheels, tyres, wings and bumpers scattered everywhere. The foreman and his three mechanics were exhausted as a result of the intensive search.

'The thing is – I don't think we've got a manual for this particular model,' said the foreman, sitting on a stool and drinking tea.

'So, how are we going to put it back together?' asked one of the mechanics.

'That could be very tricky, but I'm sure we'll manage.'

'It's like putting together a jigsaw puzzle, isn't it?'

'That'll be all part of the fun of it.'

'Incidentally,' said the mechanic, 'the chassis number doesn't even tally with the vehicle document.'

'So what else is new,' said the foreman in a resigned manner.

Terry carried a pint and a half of lager to a table, where he sat down. Bridget picked up the pint and Terry, with an embarrassed smile took the half. A fiddler was on a small platform in the corner, playing a lilting romantic air.

'I really like you, Terry,' said Bridget laying her hand over Terry's. 'Have you got a steady girl-friend?'

'Not really. Is this a proposition?'

'You never know. Maybe you're too old for me. I'm only nineteen. Anyway – what do you do?'

'Not a lot,' he replied. 'You could say I'm self employed.'

'You mean, you're on the dole?'

'Certainly not,' said Terry , looking affronted. 'Look – I've had ordinary jobs. And plenty of guys would be happy to get any kind of job. But it's not for me. Some people think I'm pretty hard – being an ex-fighter and all that. But really, I'm for the soft options. I've no qualifications – except my fists – I don't want to punch a card, so what else can I do? I get by – that's all.'

'I think you need a good woman. Get yourself together. Hey, I know what, there's a job at the hospital – boilerman.'

Terry looked at her. 'Boilerman?'

'Lots of opportunities –'

'Like what?' Terry asked bleakly.

'Central heating fitter.'

'That's very nice of you, Bridget – I really need that –'

Back at the police station, Rycott was talking on the phone when a gloomy Klingmann took out a bottle of whisky and poured out two liberal measures into plastic cups. Rycott put down the phone and stared at Klingmann as he gave him the cup. Rycott swallowed and gasped. 'I usually have it with water.'

'I like soda – the English style,' said Klingmann.

'Yeah – well it's not the Ritz.' Then he began to berate Klingmann, who became more and more bewildered as he listened. 'I should've known – he's going to shout blue murder, just when I had him banged to rights.

'Forgive me – I do not understand,' protested Klingmann.

'D'you know, I can't even nick him on the car? Fraudulent logbook – what's that, eh? He hasn't even sold the car yet. It's times like this when I think about leaving the force. The humiliation. I don't think I can face Arthur. Do you think you could talk to him –?' Rycott looked up at Klingmann with all the fervour of a desperate man.

Bridget was still trying to convince Terry to take an ordinary job. 'I know what . . . why don't you open a little dry cleaner's shop?'

'You've got some great ideas, haven't you?'

'Just helping –'

Suddenly MacFadyen loomed over them. 'What's he doing here?' he asked menacingly, looking at Terry.

'We're discussing dry cleaning –' Bridget smiled up at him.

'Frank,' said Terry, 'I didn't have a chance to talk to you –'

'After my money, aren't you?'

'Look – Arthur's in the nick.'

'I'm not surprised.'

'They reckon that car you sold him was carrying some – you know – well, drugs.'

'Are you accusing me –'

'No, but obviously they want to talk to you.'

'Yeah. And then they're going to fit me up.'

'Look, it's probably –' said Terry cautiously.

'What?'

'Well, I don't know –' His voice trailed away.

'And what have you been saying?' he said to Bridget.

Bridget was annoyed. 'Don't you start at me, Frank. I can handle him any day,' she said to Terry.

Then he tried again. 'Look – please come down with me to the nick. It's just a misunderstanding. It'll only take ten minutes; I've got a motor round the corner.'

'And then what? I go with you and somebody else is going to mug me. All you cockneys are a bit fly.'

'Come on, Frank.' Terry stood up.

'Save it,' said MacFadyen and with sudden dexterity, he hit Terry on the jaw. For the second time that day, he went down.

'I'll tell your father about you,' MacFadyen said to Bridget. 'You're hanging around with the wrong people.' He didn't wait for an answer and turned, barging through the crowd.

'I thought you were good,' said Bridget to Terry, who was getting up groggily.

'He's done it again,' he muttered and then rushed to the door, pushing other people out of the way, and staggered out into the street.

When MacFadyen saw that Terry was after him he started running across the street and on to a passing bus. He stood on the platform, giving Terry a cheery wave, confident that he would never catch him now.

The bus accelerated and then stopped at a set of traffic signals as the lights changed from amber to red. By this time, Terry was a hundred yards behind the bus, his arms pumping, his teeth gritted. The lights changed from red to amber. MacFadyen looked worried, for Terry was now only a few yards behind the bus. The driver engaged gear, the bus lurched and Terry grabbed the rail. He was breathless and the conductor looked at him in amazement as he started up the stairs. MacFadyen was ready for him and kicked out as he reached the top, but Terry grabbed the rail and heaved himself on to the upper deck. MacFadyen momentarily lost his balance as the bus took a corner and Terry flung himself at him and they went into an erratic clinch.

The conductor told the few passengers to get off the bus. Then he ran round to the driver. 'There's a fight,' he said.

'Any good?'

'Not bad.'

'OK – keep an eye on it and I'll drive round to the nick.'

Arthur, with tremendous martyrdom, was sitting beside a desk in the police station and signing a receipt for his personal effects. Klingmann and Rycott looked both embarrassed and disappointed.

'As you know,' said Arthur, clearing his throat, 'I'm not a vindictive man –'

'I know, Arthur,' said Rycott quickly.

'But what can I say? Are apologies in order?'

'Well, I suppose so –'

'You've been a model interviewee. I have had a long career and you are one of the best subjects I've met,' said Klingmann with heavy approval.

'That's terrific. Obviously, you will be hearing from my solicitor.'

'I thought he was shooting –'

'Not for the rest of his life. Monday, maybe –'

'You've got to understand *our* point, Mr Daley. This international fight against crime is important. Don't you agree?' asked Klingmann.

'It's a moral dilemma, innit? The safeguard of the individual or the common good of the state?'

Klingmann puffed at his pipe. 'That is a fine philosophical point –'

'I should cocoa!' said Arthur indignantly. 'I mean – you pluck a man from his fireside –'

'It was a car site,' said Rycott quickly.

'Never mind,' continued Arthur, ' a law abiding citizen, a

local personality, a man known to give to admirable charities such as old folks, children, veteran footballers on their uppers, distressed show business people, stars of yesteryear who can't have a decent lunch at the Savoy Grill anymore. Me – respected, even *loved* by some –' He suddenly looked at Rycott. 'Are you listening to me?'

'Not really,' said Rycott.

'And why not?' Arthur said furiously.

'I've heard it all before.'

The fight continued as the bus pulled up with a screech of brakes outside the police station. The driver jumped out of his cab and dashed inside. A few seconds later, six policemen ran from the station to the bus.

At the top of the stairs at least two of the officers hesitated.

'Go on then – get 'em,' yelled the Sergeant.

'You must be joking,' said one of the policemen.

Swaying, but from punch-drunkenness now, Terry and MacFadyen still fought furiously. Then Terry got MacFadyen jammed between two seats and rained blows on him. Eventually the two of them collapsed on the deck – but Terry was on top.

'You're a hard man,' MacFadyen gasped.

Terry shook his head dazedly. 'You're a bit tasty yourself,' he said and fell back.

The police then moved in.

Arthur stood on the top steps of the police station. He lit a cigar and smiled. Klingmann and Rycott stood behind him. They all watched with fascination the battered, bloodied faces of Terry and MacFadyen as they were hurried towards them by an eager cluster of policemen.

'What's happening, eh?' asked Arthur lazily.

Terry freed himself for a moment. 'I've got him,' he said proudly. 'I've got MacFadyen!'

But Arthur was far from grateful. 'Where have you been? Never mind *him*. You left me on my own.' He drew on his cigar proudly, mentally hearing a burst of martial music. 'It was *me* against them. And you were no help. I've had a result. I'm out.'

'Well, you were innocent anyway.'

'Yeah, but they didn't know that!'

Terry turned to Rycott. 'What about me, Mr Rycott?'

'It's not down to me,' he said. 'He's *out* – you're *in*. Different case – a public disturbance, malicious damager to property, GBH? We'll think of something.'

'Arthur – tell 'em,' said Terry desperately.

But Arthur was preoccupied. 'Look I've got to go home to have a bath and a decent drink. I've had a very traumatic time.'

The police began to push Terry towards the entrance.

'Yeah, but I did this for you –'

'All right, all right. But you've got to fight 'em, Terry. Like me, fight 'em.'

Terry gave a bitter glance. 'I've gone right off you, Arthur,' he said as the door of the police station banged behind him.

'You'll be all right,' Arthur called after Terry. Then he smiled at Klingmann and Rycott. 'He's a good lad,' said Arthur, 'in his heart of hearts.' He walked slowly down the steps to the street.

Arthur was away and Rycott looked regretfully after him. Still, he promised himself, there would be another time. There *must* be.

Having shaved, bathed and washed his hair, Arthur went down to the Winchester for a quick one. He still felt exhausted and, however much he had washed and sprayed himself with deodorant, Arthur still felt he had the sour smell of the prison cell on him.

'What's up Arthur?' Dave was solicitous, vaguely kind and Arthur felt moved, almost to tears. It was so good to see a friendly face, to receive a pleasant word.

'An unfortunate misunderstanding,' said Arthur closing his eyes and sipping his large vodka. It was like nectar.

'Yeah – I heard about that. All over a motor wasn't it?'

Arthur opened his eyes, hissing sharply at Dave. 'It's a closed book now.'

'Is it?'

'It's not the kind of experience that I want to talk about, Dave – I think you have to understand that. I mean – a man in my position isn't used to that kind of experience and it takes a little time to recover.'

Dave shook his head sympathetically. 'I can understand that Arthur.'

'It's played on my nerves. Shaken me up.'

'Have one on the house, Arthur.'

'Well –'

'Go on – it'll do you good.'

'I'll accept a gift,' said Arthur, 'and it's good of you.'

'You've had a rough time, Arthur.'

Arthur sighed. 'You can say that again.'

'You've had –'

'All right, Dave. Don't get waggish. My recovery is going to be slow – I mean – I could be having a nervous breakdown.' Arthur took another long draft of vodka. 'I can feel the colour coming back to my cheeks, Dave. I'm losing the stir pallor.'

'I thought you were white, Arthur.'

'White? I was ashen.'

'Arthur –' Dave spoke after a full minute of restful silence.

'Yes?' His voice was soporific, unencouraging.

'I hear Terry's in there now.'

Arthur stared at him blankly. 'Yes?'

'Terry, Arthur. He's in there.'

'So I gather.'

'Anything you can do for him?'

'Me?' Arthur sounded outraged.

'Well – is there?'

'What can I do? He got himself into a fight on the bus. The situation's out of my hands.'

'Wasn't it connected with this car business?' Dave gently enquired and Arthur began to sweat with guilt.

'Very likely.'

'Ah – so there's nothing you can do?'

'What do you expect me to do?'

'You could go down there.'

Arthur's eyes opened wide with alarm. 'You mean – back to the nick?'

'You could just drop in,' suggested Dave hesitantly.

'Dave, you don't understand my position.'

'No.'

'My mental position.'

'Eh?'

'I've just suffered a nervous trauma by being incarcerated. I'm in no fit state to go back.'

'It's like getting back on a horse again.'

'What?'

Dave counselled him patiently. 'If you fall off a horse, you've got to get back on again.'

'Why?'

'To get your confidence back.'

'What do you want your confidence back for? I don't like horses.'

'Arthur –'

'I wouldn't be on one.'

'It's a figure of speech.'

'What have horses got to do with the nick, Dave. Are you out of your tiny?' Arthur looked at him with mounting concern. 'You're rambling.'

'What I'm trying to say, Arthur,' said Dave speaking slowly and carefully, 'is that if you walk back inside that nick you'll feel better.'

'Will I?'

'Bound to.'

'Why?'

'Because – if you walk inside that nick, you can bail Terry out.'

'Why should I do that?'

'Because you owe him one,' said Dave. He took out a ledger. 'Like you owe me twenty sovs.'

Arthur gave him a sickly smile. 'You mean I should take

my courage in both hands?'

'Take in what you like, Arthur,' said Dave leaning intently over the bar, 'but I still tell you – you owe him one.'

'Arthur – fancy seeing you again so quickly.' Rycott stood welcomingly in the foyer of the police station.

'I'm on business.' Arthur looked around him nervously.

'Trying to sell us something? Another Merc?'

'Very amusing, Mr Rycott.'

'You look nervous, Arthur. You don't find the atmosphere oppressive in here, do you?'

'Where's the Gestapo?'

'Herr Klingmann's time with us is over. He's gone back to his mother country.'

'Back to Colditz, eh?'

'Düsseldorf, actually.'

'Same thing.'

'Well – what can we do for you?' Rycott smiled helpfully. 'Come to confess have you?'

'I beg your pardon?'

'To any misdeeds.'

'I take that in poor part, Mr Rycott. As you may know – I've just been cleared of a grievous charge. This has affected my nerves and my business.'

'What do you want, Arthur?'

'I've come to bail out Terry.'

'Ah.'

'Well?' Arthur looked at Rycott quizzically.

'I'm not sure that's possible.'

'What do you mean?' asked Arthur suspiciously.

'We're charging him with a serious affray.'

'I'm sure in the circumstances you owe me,' stated Arthur firmly.

'I beg your pardon?'

But Arthur was firm. 'You owe me one, Mr Rycott.'

Back in the Winchester, Terry and Arthur drank to freedom. Dave was also in a jovial mood, although he didn't seem ready to offer as many drinks on the house as Arthur considered would justify a celebration. However, despite this slight shadow, Arthur was magnanimous when Terry asked:

'What kept you, Arthur?'

'I could have asked you the same question, old son.'

'When?'

'When I was in stir, Terry. When I was in chokey and waiting, wondering about outside assistance.'

'You took your time.'

'Dave will tell you I had to overcome my nerves, Terry.'

'Your *what*?'

'Dave – give Terence an idea of the state I was in.'

'Arthur was in a bad state, Terry.'

'What kind of state?' asked Terry unbelievingly.

'My nerves,' said Arthur. 'But I had to mount the horse again.'

'What horse?'

'If you fall off a horse, Terry, you have to get back on again.'

'Since when did you take up riding horses, Arthur?'

'It's a play on words. A speakeasy.'

Terry and Dave looked at him, both completely mystified.

'I had to regain my confidence to cross the threshold. Once done – I came galloping to you on my steed.'

'How many vodkas have you had, Arthur?' asked Terry.

But Arthur ignored him. 'You should be grateful, Terry.'

'I'm grateful, Arthur.'

Dave sighed. 'So it's a real reunion, is it?' he asked wonderingly.

'Is it?' asked Terry.

'We've got a great future, you and I, Terence,' pronounced Arthur. 'We're going a long way.'

Terry put a hand to his battered face. 'I feel I've been a long way already,' he said.

Minder

A NOVEL BY ANTHONY MASTERS

Based on the popular television series

TERRY AND ARTHUR ARE BACK!

ARTHUR:

'My word is my bond. And I'll let Terry fight to the death to prove it.'

TERRY:

'Not that I'd call Arthur mean, but when you have a drink with him he just buys the crisps!'

Arthur's the one with the silver tongue, he could talk his way past St. Peter if he wanted to. Terry's the rented muscle, the one Arthur uses to do the tidying up. Trouble is, for Terry and Arthur there's usually a sting in the tail . . .

TV TIE-IN 0 7221 5824 6 £1.50